TONE ON TONE/ OF ALL THAT IS:

The spiritual autobiography of Kenneth Grahame

TONE ON TONE/OF ALL THAT IS: the spiritual autobiography of Kenneth Grahame

This is a work of fiction. All of the characters, names, incidents, organizations, and dialogue in this novel are either the products of the author's imagination or are used fictitiously.

iUniverse books may be ordered through booksellers or by contacting:

iUniverse LLC
1663 Liberty Drive
Bloomington, IN 47403
www.iuniverse.com
1-800-Authors (1-800-288-4677)

ISBN: 978-1-4759-5817-1 (sc)
ISBN: 978-1-4759-5822-5 (e)

Printed in the United States of America.

iUniverse rev. date: 11/05/2013

TONE ON TONE/ OF ALL THAT IS:

The spiritual autobiography of Kenneth Grahame

NATHAN POLLACK

iUniverse LLC
Bloomington

TONE ON TONE
ΤΩΝ ΟΝΤΩΝ
by Nathan Pollack

TONE ON TONE

ΤΩΝ ΟΝΤΩΝ

"OF ALL THERE IS . . ." ARISTOTLE (PHYSICS, Book II)

Note: The title of this story is <u>Tone on Tone</u> especially because it is the closest transliteration of the first two words of the Greek text of the Second Book of Aristotle's Physics. The phrase in English suggests an important aspect of this many-faceted story, that just as music cannot be pure tone, but must be tone on tone in a moment of time (harmony) and in sequence in time (melody), life cannot be pure joy, pure sorrow or pure sanity. "Των οντων" is not especially easy to translate. By itself it means something like "Of all that is . . ." or "Of all that exists . . ." Aristotle goes on to separate those things on the one hand which by nature develop, function, reproduce (perhaps) and decay, as distinct from, on the other hand, those artifacts of man which are (literally) unnatural. Among those latter Aristotle and I include society and all institutions. Tone on tone, layer upon layer, full brilliant spectrum, mixed emotions—these are motifs of true life experience I try to touch deeply in this frothy fantasy. Now I see this story much more thoroughly than when it started to write itself, and it has become, indeed <u>TONE ON TONE/OF ALL THAT IS: the spiritual autobiography of Kenneth Grahame.</u>

Thank you again.

NMP
Denver, Colorado
December 14, 1990

Walk the aisles of the office supply store. Here is something new, a portable word processor, a StarWriter. Who has that much money? I spend it first, then find it. With this I could write anywhere there is an electric plug. A bargain at $600.00. The handle makes it portable if not light, so I carry it to the car and into the bar. The coffee bar, for I have been sober for some time.

I feared I would write nothing sober, that my creative life was over. How could I act out the agonies of my childhood hero Edgar Allan Poe if I stopped drinking? But the pain had become too shattering to endure. Poe was dead by my age and I was not. I cheerfully gave up writing to crawl out of my grave of drunkenness, to begin living.

Truth is that I had never sold a word, never had a reader. But I had written quite a bit. The art I pursued then and now is what is called the art of medicine (I call it science, but that is another distraction; you probably call it art). The energy I focused on getting sober those days hardly left me time between midnight and three to dive into the gloom Poe and I had drunk interminably. I was satisfied enough to awaken each morning, write in my journal, "The sun rose bright and so did I."

I was anxious to examine my new StarWriter. Muddy's Java Café was dark mid-afternoon. It was empty except for Rae the coffee-bartender. She wiped tables from the lunch crowd. I searched for an electric outlet, none to be found. She let me use the one behind the bar, so I set my machine on the bar, turned it on. Slowly the green glow coalesced; there was a shallow screen—how many lines? I'd have to try, then count.

I typed at random, automatic you might call it. Rae walked by, glanced over my shoulder, said, "'Inner child . . .' We were just talking about that this morning." I looked. Sure enough, the term "inner child" was in that paragraph I had jotted mindlessly. The screen held eight lines.

"Inner child . . ." A manic middle-aged man searches for his inner child, finds him. Good. All thought is wordplay. Every story I ever wrote was based on a bad pun.

Of all that is, some is by nature, some contrived. That's the sort of thing Aristotle said in Physics, as I recall. Some time early in the writing of this story I began to have a sense of seeking what is natural, what is really real. A lot like getting sober. So this was my first sober writing.

What isn't "natural"? Well, everything in the world is natural, way beyond the puny limits of our imagination. But we humans, at least I, contrive the most narrow brittle perverted things—greed for more, expectations of what is inconceivable, revenge on others. What conceits we contrive are just what we have a yearning to be freed of. So, how can we stop contriving pain and destruction out of our insatiable greed-for-everything that turns to ashes? How can we allow to emerge in our world what comes to be without our contriving, naturally?

I couldn't. It was very slow, learning to "go with the flow". So without trying I was blessed with the assignment to write a story, an example of how to shift perspective from the busy narrow termite nest of the city to immenseness of all that is, ALL that is.

Contents

(Summary, Dialogue Samples and Cinema Suggestions).........xiii

A Conversation Between A Man And A Boy
1. Unsure 1
2. It Is A Wood 3
3. Tree-Like 5
4. Run 6
5. Skittering Down The Scree 8
6. Necessity 10
7. In Ways No Animal Will 12
8. An Old Purse 15
9. Conversation With A Stranger 16
10. Calmer 19
11. Float Or Fly.. 20
12. Recapitulate 23
13. The Center 26
14. The Carnival 28
15. Curiouser And Curiouser.....................................31
16. The Devil's Den 33
17. Monica... 35
18. Rick 37
19. The Chilton 39
20. Approaching The Boy 44
21. Time Together To Speak 46

A Quietness Between A Man And Himself
1. Serenity...53
2. Balsam Boughs...55
3. Snow...57

4. Frozen...59

5. Now Is The Time..61

6. I Am Not He...64

7. Questions Pendant...66

8. Free To Speak..69

9. Silver Space-Ships...70

10. I Wonder..72

11. Empathy...74

12. Twin Specks..78

13. Real Coffee...80

A Raucous Conversation Among A Man And Himselves

1. We Are Five.......................................83

2. The Wind In The Willows 86

3. Waiting...89

4. The Wind 92

5. The Wake 96

6. Precipitously To Descend 98

7. We Wait...101

8. Goodies 104

9. Rattling And Lurching 107

10. Knotted Self................................112

11. What I Want 115

12. Whispers 117

13. Species And Subspecies 120

14. Hot Dogs 123

15. This Tragedy...............................127

16. Excited..131

17. A Moment Is The Pivot................134

18. Make Yourselves At Home 136

19. The Last Cassowary.....................139

20. A Wonderful Banquet...................143

Learning To Listen, Listening To Learn

1. I Walk..151

2. Whatever 154

3. Re-Enter Society 157

4. A Monument...161

5. Welcome 163
6. Ghost...167
7. Pure Energy..170
8. Wonder 172
9. Handsome 174
10. Clothing Which Almost Fits 177
11. Did You Have Sex? 181
12. Deep Joy.. 183
13. Whoopsie! 185
14. Midnight.. 190
15. Together 193

Tone on Tone

(Summary, Dialogue Samples and Cinema Suggestions)

DRAMATIS PERSONAE

Section I	Section II	Section III	Section IV
Kenneth Grahame (Suffering Self [ego]):			
a banker	a survivor	an author in his own mind	simply a man, a simple man
The Wise Old One (Reassuring Self [superego]):			
an old Indian, Kenneth's spiritual guide	an old Indian, Pongo's spiritual guide	Ms. Badger	Madge, *mater familias*
The Inner Child:			
Pongo Bernoulli, boy prostitute	Pongo, a boy	Moley	Pongo, a growing boy
Impulsive Self (Id):			
Monica, a hooker	the unseen, long-awaited *femme fatale*	Monica Toad	Monica, a whole woman, Kenneth's lover
Intellect (Adolescent Self [observing ego]):			
Rick, a pimp	the Student	Ratty	Rick, a serious young man
Red, a drunk			Red, a sobering drunk

. . . and Yuppies, Bums, Sigmund Freud, the ghost of Aristotle, Hookers, a Bartender, a Waitress, Bikers, Hunter S. Thompson, a Cassowary, a few Swans, many Ducks, *et alii*.

Summary

Kenneth, a middle-age banker, has burnt out. He seeks some contact with his inner child lest he explode and die. Pragmatic throughout his forty years, uncharacteristically he does not question inexplicable events nor defend against their dangers. He follows where he is led—from a mountaintop, to the mountain meadow, to the plain where he encounters bikers, to the city where he was born (which has become impersonal to him), to the center of the city's vice, to the embodiment of his inner child (a boy prostitute). Kenneth is killed by the boy's pimp. **[End Section I]**, but immediately is in the mountain meadow again awaiting the boy. The wait he expected to be an hour or a day extends through the entire winter, during which he faces death again—cold and starvation. None the less he is alive as spring comes, and with it comes a youth who could be the boy grown older. They await others whom the man does not know. His lifelong spiritual guide, and companion of his recent adventures, brings the small boy. The four of them await one more. As his emaciated isolated self is drinking these persons in like spring sunshine, he turns to them and they have become animals (Muppets). **[End Section II]** The long-awaited Monica Toad flamboyantly arrives, and a second trip down the mountain ensues, during which love, acceptance and mutual support are confirmed among these five (Kenneth Grahame, Toad, Badger, Mole and Rat). His animal companions recede into his fantasy as he is suddenly alone in the reality of the city without friends or resources. **[End Section III]** He begins panhandling, gradually and accidentally makes acquaintances. Because he is more honest with himself, more accepting than he was, his life is simpler. He carries the equanimity his animal friends (newly discovered aspects of his inner self) lovingly have brought him. By chance he encounters the father of the man accused of murdering him, helps to free the younger man, and eventually joins this group of pimps and prostitutes to rebuild the dilapidated hotel in which he previously had been killed. Their acceptance and mutual support, their active collaboration in concrete work (rather than dependence and exploitation) make them a real family. In the final scene of this story they are going to the mountain meadow for a picnic, the camera closing on a vista of the Rockies at sunset, the broadest view of the mountains yet in Kenneth's three (or four) allegoric journeys thence [**which ends the fourth and final section**].

<u>Scenes and Dialogue</u>

Scene: Throughout the first of the four sections of this movie the camera does not visualize the main character, although his monologues and dialogues are heard. The opening view is from high up in the corner of a psychiatrist's office looking down, centering on the psychiatrist's head as he sits in a dark red leather wing chair, legs crossed, unmoving, note pad in his left hand, Mont Blanc fountain pen in his right. Of the couch the back and edge can be seen, and perhaps the tips of Kenneth's highly polished Italian wing tips. The view is so distant that even though the psychiatrist in his large chair and the even larger couch are in the very center, one's eye first is brought to circle all the dark, deep rich color of oriental carpets, floor to ceiling bookshelves of dark polished wood filled with leather-bound volumes, tall plants in jardinieres, all these dark richnesses illuminated by bright sunlight coming from an unseen window. The initial still-life is held long enough to allow the audience to wonder if the psychiatrist is alive or merely the wax stereotype of Freud—white hair, white goatee, tweeds, carved pipe on the table beside him. After the long moment of silent stillness, the zoom is slowly in as the monologue begins. The zoom in continues smoothly until it focuses on the psychiatrist's carved-ivory hands, the pen, the tablet. Finally there is a slight movement of the fingers of the right hand to make a minuscule mark on the pad. As the monologue continues, the camera pans about the room in a changing, almost random pattern, focusing on each rich item—occasional tables and the lamps on them, the richly colored carpet, a turned newel post, plants in Chinese porcelain jardinieres, a glass-topped case filled with small Egyptian artifacts. Finally the camera comes, in its continuous motion, to the bookshelves, scans slowly from left to right a series of book spines the order of whose titles and authors tells some preposterous tale (or, better yet, the credits for the movie).

<u>Kenneth</u>: I had a dream. I dreamed I saw a little boy, the saddest and most silent little boy who ever was. Not only did I feel, but knew he is real, communicating with me through my disturbed dreaming. I must speak with him, but even if I find him I won't know how to begin the conversation. Somehow I realize the conversation is much older than I am, and knowing it makes me feel older, much older. And there seems no way to communicate because I have forgotten the meaning of what I seek, the meaning of my own life. It is important to me now to remember this is a meaning I have known once, but somehow I have lost my conscious cosmic rootedness in it. In my soul I am convinced that I smelled, tasted and knew the meaning when I was a child. Every one must. I have insisted to myself that they knew no better—the grownups. I have transcended my bitterness by losing my senses, becoming numb. I was taught that big people knew the truth, that their knowledge gave them authority over me. Now I know they knew no better than what they did and how they did it, all words and titles aside. I certainly know no better than they did. I brutalized my own children, overpowered my wives and employees. I'm afraid I have brutalized, silenced and isolated my own child within. Now I want to open negotiations with him, show good faith, ask him to help me live. Before I can ask for forgiveness I must forgive myself. My acceptance of the adults and authorities in my life for who they are—that they know no better—must be authentic, and exactly that sort of acceptance I must offer myself also. Before I can approach my own true heart I have to forgive me, I have to accept the man I am and with him accept all adult human beings in a manner kinder than I had imagined possible. It is not merely possible, but terrifyingly joyous. And I must find the child I have dreamed of, offer honestly what I can to him. I hope he will not continue hating me. I need him desperately. Well, there is nothing for me in the bank but money, nothing for me on this couch but rumination, so I must go today, now! (Frantic crescendo.)

Scene: Without losing the bright daylight, moves down New York City streets to an immense bank, through the halls, past guards, receptionists, to the Office of the Director, to the door marked with his name ("Kenneth Grahame, President"), to the opulent desk, behind which the camera sits. A small rustic water color is signed "KG." An old Indian paces before the desk (Johnny Looking Cloud).

Kenneth: It is kind of you to come with me on an uncharted journey which is likely to be painful for me, dry and tedious for you. I do not know which way to go nor how we ought be provisioned. So, immediately come! I lead you with my unknowing.

Scene: Again without losing sunlight to high up on a mountain, in trees, late summer. In all the scenes of this entire section the camera takes Kenneth's eye view, or at least will not see Kenneth. The Indian (his companion) is seen sparingly (e.g., at the creek's edge at dawn bending over the fire), but usually standing next to Kenneth (i.e., unseen by the camera). Kenneth's ruminating monologues—manic, pressured and loquacious—are voiced over scenes of calm, still mountain beauty, except when he is crashing down the mountain, at which times the camera drags the audience also, as if down a roller-coaster. Later in the section when other characters are encountered and dialogue ensues, those persons intrude into the whole screen, perhaps through the distorted intrusiveness of a fish-eye lens.

Kenneth: This is a wood. I am not surprised. I anticipated a place severe and cold (but I am never truly prepared for what is really painful). I am relieved. I say relieved, not pleased, because to me pleasure comes from what I am and what I do—to be pleased with myself. Placation, not pleasure, is what comes from what you do for me, your attempts to please me (as if you ever could). Relief is objective, realistic—that I do not suffer the freezing and the beating which I feared. This is a wood. I am relieved. Air is warm, even shadows. The air is alive not with writhing teeming insects and the fetid invisible mist of rotting biota, but air, modest and unveiled, gives out each of the discrete smells of the wood's beings. Even I can distinguish balsam, spruce, grasses' dusts, flowers whose names I do not know, moss and mud and moistness of this shaded stream whose odors clearly sing to my nose exactly who a spring is, but no more clearly than its living self is sung to my ears by its gurgling kindly voice or even its reverberating relationship to me bespoken by the sound of my feet springily squishing at the water's edge (reinforced by the proprioception—my feeling of myself in my own parts—of my ankles' movements minusculely waving on the gelid ocean of this foot-wide band of mulch-covered mud) . . . And the vision! Beings, shapes and movements, colors, changes of colors—all coordinated with the sounds and smells as if in an intricately edited movie, each sensation of which has told the whole story, and all together very much a symphony (but symphony means sounds together and this is everything together here and now in all senses named and unnamable) and all together touching me, because I also am here, and more amazing magic that I also am a part of it, and make smells in stirring air which I am stirring, and I eat all this in and I live and I am nourished, and happily I can recline here to be devoured by all that is about me, to be fed by and to feed the universe, the symphony. I am real. This is a wood. I sense it is familiar to me. I am at home outdoors. In cities I am alone and lost. Shall I believe terrifying tales of the consumption of innocents lost in the woods? Is it not the terrifying tale itself which destroys innocence? Even I have felt uncannily at home on a mountain, in a field, at the beach picking through the shells and pebbles huge Ocean offers me as I weavingly dance in and out the edge of her surf whose waning froth caresses my feet and toes (usually dry, covered parts of me in shoes, not moved, not shown, not shared), surf churning sand like fragrant steaming coffee grounds. The part of me which must succeed would be ashamed to get lost, but the part of me which needs to live and grow must be free to wander without fear of wandering. If there is a part of me which wishes to survive, shall I hide it under armor, or leave it loose to wander? I know where we are! Don't ask me how till later. Now follow me. We'll get along somehow. It may be a long way and a long time before we are back here—maybe never—but we must be here now and move along with no guarantee of anything.

Don't worry. I feel better about all this each moment. Don't trust me—trust all of life. Thanks for being with me. I can't reciprocate in any concrete way, but I do thank you. Come!

(Crash downhill, trees flying past, to the clearing of the mountain meadow where they spend a night.)

*   *   *

Scene: Down the mountain and onto the plain, the two companions encounter about a hundred bikers, ballerinas and Hunter S. Thompson (played by Hunter S. Thompson).

Biker: Why you traveling this way?

Kenneth: 'This way'? Do you mean 'in this fashion' or 'in this direction'?

Biker: Both the How and the Tao.

Kenneth: Wow! You appear a criminal drunken devilish wild man, but you make subtle discriminations. And you are not drunk, despite appearances.

Biker: I don't drink any more.

Kenneth: How come?

Biker: You know my story. They're all about the same, really.

Kenneth: How do *you* get here?

Biker: By my bike. And where do *you* think you're going?

Kenneth: You know my agenda. They're all about the same, really.

Biker: (matter-of-factly) You are looking for yourself, and the deeper you go the loster you get. You seem frantic trying to master the mountain, which has quickly cast you off. You seem frightened trying to meet people. You have some idea of what you want to do, but you refuse to understand that you can't do it. It must be done for you, and that will come when you are ready, and it won't be anything like what you have planned or imagined.

Kenneth: Can I trust you?

Biker: Can you? Who is more trustworthy than a stranger? How can I harm you, other than to kill you? I certainly won't gossip about you, 'cause I don't care about you, and I don't know any of your family or friends, and you probably don't have any friends left anyhow. You have no reason to care what I think of you, do you?

Kenneth: No, I suppose I don't. But if you don't care and if I don't care, why do I want to tell you about me, and why are you willing to hear me?

Biker: Because I have been heard, so now again I hear. Being heard won't fix you, but go ahead. I'm listening.

*   *   *

Scene: Arduously Kenneth and his companion make their way to the city, to the center of the city, to the slums of the center of the city and to the basement dives of the slums of the center of the city. Kenneth is instructed by Red to find Rick (Pongo's pimp) in order to find the boy. Kenneth finds it incredible that the boy is a prostitute, denies what Red has told him. They are at The Devil's Den, a loud low dive.

Monica: Looking for someone, Good Looking?

Kenneth: Huh?

Monica: I'm Monica. Come sit with me. Come. Right here on the stool next to me so I can look at you.

<u>Kenneth:</u> Oh, okay. I just happened in, just came to look around.

<u>Monica:</u> Until you saw me.

<u>Kenneth:</u> Until I saw you, and came to sit with you.

<u>Monica:</u> Buy me a drink.

<u>Kenneth:</u> Okay, I'll buy you a drink, but I don't want you to misunderstand. I have an important errand. I really don't have time to visit.

<u>Monica:</u> Oh, so you think I'm only interested in one thing. Well, I'm not. I'll be glad just to visit for a while, so make yourself at home. Do you think I'm beautiful?

<u>Kenneth:</u> (To himself, voice over, *à la* Marlowe or Spade) I could see Monica was beautiful even before I could see anything else in this crowded darkness. Now all I can see is more of her beauty. But why such beauty in a whore? I do not blame her for how she is, but why she is that way. She is white, all white. She is long and pale. Her dress is white eyelet and taffeta, puffed at the shoulders and dipped at the breast. (Her breasts are pale as marshmallows. I see and almost smell the warm dry softness of their sugar powder surface as she dips to pick up her carefully dropped handkerchief.) Her hair is silver white, and in her hand she holds the white lace handkerchief which sketches vapor trails in the dark as she freely gesticulates pointing to herself, opening her arms away to the distant unseen sky, bringing her hands back to her breast. [*to her he says*] Oh, yes, you are beautiful, Monica.

<u>Monica:</u> You're not so bad yourself. What is this terrible errand you must do, rather than to spend some time with me?

<u>Kenneth:</u> No one seems to understand, and I am beginning to understand why. I am looking for a boy I hope is here. I have come to feel incomplete without him, but the only way I know to look to find him is to follow my intuitive impulses. I am a very practical

and rational man—at least I was—and I don't understand what I am going to do, but I must do it. Does that make any sense to you?

Monica: No. But don't let that worry you, Honey. You just go find that boy. And if you ever get it straight and have enough time—and money—come see me.

Kenneth: I understand that you don't understand, but that will have to be okay for now. Here's twenty for the drink (I hope you get part of it), and twenty for you if you will answer a question for me: How can I find Rick?

(Cold white shoulder.)

*   *   *

Interim: Kenneth finds the boy, but is killed by the boy's pimp. The boy, a life-long mute, says, "Meet me at the mountain meadow." Again he is on the mountain, waiting for the boy, but the boy does not come. The camera has been seeing Kenneth (rather than seeing from Kenneth) from his return to the mountain, coming back to consciousness from having been killed, and throughout the winter during which Kenneth freezes, starves but survives, all in wordlessness. Now with the coming of spring a voice suddenly appears, a young man's voice.

Student: You look good in a beard.

Kenneth: I don't wear a beard, I just haven't had time to shave this winter, and . . . It's about time you came. I've missed you.

Student: And I've missed you.

Kenneth: And why am I not surprised for you so suddenly to appear, so late, and so grown up, I believe?

Student: You are not surprised and I am not surprised because we have cared enough and survived enough to take away most of our expectations, our naïveté.

Kenneth: You mean expectations are naivete?

Student: Is that what *you* mean?

Kenneth: You mean we mean the same?

Student: Probably, now.

Kenneth: Then why are we bothering to converse?

Student: Is it a bother for you?

Kenneth: No. As I said, I have missed you. I feel I have spent all my life until now trying to make contact with you. I feel I need you, and I feel you need me. I mean, more exactly, I feel incomplete without having a sense of you, and I feel obligated to care for your vulnerability.

Student: Vulnerability? Man, we need to talk.

Kenneth: Yes, thank you, that's what I mean, that we need to talk. I may not say things quite right the first try, but I know that what I mean to say is right.

Student: 'Right'? Is that the best word you can choose?

Kenneth: Boy, you are demanding.

Student: And generous. Here. This pack is filled with food.

Kenneth: Thanks, but I have plenty for both of us—and more growing all around. (Gestures.)

Student: Then we are well provided for, indeed. And now is the time, and here is the place.

Kenneth: Life begins anew each day. Thanks, Nameless. (Looks skyward.)

(They work together arranging the camp, now in the tree-house tower.)

Kenneth: I had plenty of room for me up here, and I thought there would be room enough for you also, even when I thought you were quite small.

Student: We need more.

Kenneth: And I'm sorry I didn't thank you for all the food you brought, but I was so proud that I myself had gotten everything you might need . . .

Student: 'Yourself'? 'Proud'?

Kenneth: No, not 'myself' . . . nor 'proud'. I guess I meant I was glad to be able to give you what you might need, for your sake, not mine.

Student: And you know what I need?

Kenneth: Did you come to demean me?

Student: And if I have?

Kenneth: I will learn to accept that also, for I accept you. I don't know why, but I don't know why not. It is my preconceived notion that I accept you as myself. It has not been easy to accept myself, much more arduous and repetitive than I had thought it would be, but accepting myself has let me live when I was dying (and perhaps when I was dead already). Accepting whatever is me about me has allowed me a measure of peace. I have a need to accept you, but you are difficult for me to accept. You seem critical of me, and you are not as I expected. I sought and met a mute lad who had been hurt, used, abused, whom I could help. Although I know you must be he, you seem quite different.

Student: I am not he.

(Silence of a day or two as they work to enlarge the camp, the tower.)

Kenneth: Then, who are you?

Student: You said you knew me.

Kenneth: Now I do, having worked with you in silence, having eaten with you what you brought here, having experienced within myself what my reactions are to you. Who are you?

Student: You might call me a student.

Kenneth: Are you angry at my foolishness?

Student: You are no more foolish than I; I simply have been learning to hide my foolishness behind learning.

Kenneth: (Matter-of-factly stating it as a new discovery) You are not the boy.

Student: No, although in a way I was he, as you were.

Kenneth: And was I *you*?

Student: Will I be *you*?

Kenneth: Maybe my having learned to live will help you somehow.

Student: You know I shall have to make my own way, my own errors, my own missteps along this path.

Kenneth: It is a broad path. The places I have passed which did seem difficult don't seem so looking back. I don't know that life truly is a path, but if we talk of it that way, then it is the path of truth. I think of the little boy, how I would like to carry him along that path—and this wish is for me, to care for something in me, to carry myself along the path safe.

Student: You do understand why I do not like that?

Kenneth: Sure, now I do. You resent generosity which is merely a guise for selfishness. You say, 'Do me no favors, especially if they are favors for yourself.'

Student: Like a writer offering to read you his stuff.

Kenneth: Do you think that's why the boy is silent?

Student: He wants to be important to you. When all you want to do is give him things, do him favors, he fears he can do nothing for you. He's afraid you want to buy him off, to silence him.

Kenneth: Doesn't he know he is the most important person of all, the most naïvely sensitive, that without him our sensations and sensitivities are coarse? Doesn't he know he is beautiful however he is, but most beautiful laughing and running? Doesn't he know for me to see him happy will convince me I was not bruised to silence when I was very young?

Student: No. Of course he does not see things as you see them, nor as I do. I also will like to see him happy, but I am the more likely to remind him life is cruel, encourage him to keep up his silent act, deep tearless eyes, to suffer everything the callous sadists offer so they won't flare angry at passive defiance and kill him outright. I beg my baby brother stay alive. I love him!

Kenneth: (With feeling.) How do you come to trust me enough to express these feelings wildly as a thicket growing thorny vines up and around each other tall as trees?

Student: To protect the baby rose.

(More building, cooking, eating, sleeping . . . and the conversation continues until the others arrive. Those four take the forms of Muppets: a little boy **mole**, a **badger** with the face and hair of Johnny Looking Cloud, the student who takes the form of a **water rat**, and the most glamorous **toad** in the western hemisphere.)

*   *   *

Camped by the river, after supper unheard whispers flit about like clouds of gnats.

Mole: She wants what?

Rat: The last cassowary.

Badger: She wants what?

Rat: The last cassowary.

Badger: I heard that, but what is a cassowary?

Rat: It's a bird.

Badger: She wants a what?

Rat: I thought you said you heard me.

Badger: I heard you, but . . . a bird?

Rat: It's a big bird.

Kenneth: Why does she want the last cassowary?

Rat: I don't know.

Kenneth: The *last* cassowary?

Rat: I guess so. She said so.

Badger: Is it the *very* last cassowary?

Rat: I don't know.

Mole: Isn't there another cassowary?

Rat: I don't know.

Mole: I mean, can't there be a special cassowary just for Toady?

Rat: I don't know.

Badger: What does she want to do with a cassowary?

Rat: I don't know.

Mole: Maybe she wants it for a pet.

Kenneth: I doubt it.

Mole: Couldn't she want it for a pet?

Badger: Can you imagine Toady taking care of a pet?

Mole: But, a little bird in a cage . . .

Rat: Four feet tall, twenty stone and able to eviscerate a man in a single kick.

Mole: Large cage?

Kenneth: No cage. No pet.

Rat: . . . Feathers?

Kenneth: Feathers.

<u>Badger:</u> Oh, no!

<u>Kenneth:</u> I'm afraid so, or something like that.

<u>Badger:</u> How can we stop her?

<u>Rat:</u> Have you ever stopped her doing anything?

<u>Badger:</u> I can't stop her, but maybe all of us together . . .

<u>Kenneth:</u> I don't think so. We can't flip switches in her head. We can't lock her up or tie her down. We've tried that before. It doesn't work.

<u>Badger:</u> We can't let her do this . . . but we can't stop her from doing this. What can we do?

<u>Kenneth:</u> We can get some sleep. We are not at the city yet. Something will happen . . . a broken axle, a snowstorm, a migration of cassowaries . . . anything but . . .

<u>Rat:</u> . . . anything but a change of heart or mind in our beloved Toady. She is a gem—obdurate as a diamond.

*   *   *

The animals evaporate and Kenneth is in the city alone. He happens upon Red at the Chilton Hotel, as he looks for a place to sleep late at night after his first job of his new life—unloading a carload of bags of cement. Red had directed Kenneth to Rick, the boy's pimp. Kenneth doesn't know Red is Rick's father. Rick stabbed Kenneth to death at the end of the first section. It is now the middle of the fourth (and last) section of this story.

<u>Red:</u> I don't recognize you. How do you know me?

<u>Kenneth:</u> Oh, you did me a favor a few months ago, gave me directions when I was lost.

<u>Red:</u> I still can't place you, to be honest. Did you have that beard then?

<u>Kenneth:</u> No, come to think of it, I didn't. I forgot I have a beard this year. I don't have to look at me, you know.

<u>Red:</u> Well, shave it, then. Give an old man an even break.

(Kenneth bathes and shaves while Red prepares some food for him.)

<u>Red:</u> So you're the guy! Am I glad to see you!

<u>Kenneth:</u> But we just met for a moment. How could you remember or care . . . ?

<u>Red:</u> You have saved my life—or saved my boy's life.

<u>Kenneth:</u> I don't understand what you are saying.

<u>Red:</u> That's not important. I understand what I am seeing.

<u>Kenneth:</u> You are happy to see me. When I walked into this room you were burdened, weighted down with something painful, your face down, your shoulders round, your step a shuffle, mumbling in a muffled voice despite an openness and kindness unlike the brashness I remember in you when we earlier met. But you were drunk then.

<u>Red:</u> And that was my last drink, at least to today. I hope never to take another.

<u>Kenneth:</u> Something dramatic must have happened then. Something dramatic happened to me, too, but I don't know how it could have touched you. Some coincidence . . . ?

<u>Red:</u> It was some coincidence, all right, and now that you show up, somehow I almost understand it. I guess it can't hurt to let you know, if . . .

<u>Kenneth:</u> If . . . ?

<u>Red:</u> Look, I may not be thinking very well, but I feel okay about you. Were you really looking for a room downstairs? Why? Why are you here, this place, this time?

<u>Kenneth:</u> This is just where I got to. I don't know why.

<u>Red:</u> And all the beds were full downstairs, so that brought you up here to me. Amazing. It just shows me again that I don't know a whole hell of a lot. I thought I was smart, and I was just drunk. I thought I was in charge of half the county, and I couldn't even remember to zip my own fly. Well, one thing that happened is I found a better way. When they arrested Rick for murder I was too stunned to take another drink. For days I just sat here stunned and angry. I told my lawyers to get him right out of there, and when they said they couldn't I was stymied. I sat here and didn't drink. For the first time in forty years I sat here staring angry holes in that wall without a bottle. When I unfroze I went to jail to see him and tried to bail him out, but they wanted more than I could get hold of—and I ain't poor. I left the jail and wandered, lost. I wandered into a meeting—I don't know how. I guess I knew all along wherever there was a church basement there had to be a meeting, that I was bound to get there some day. I'm sure at some time I had been drunk with every man and woman in that room. (I wondered where they'd gone.) They understood more about what was happening to me than I did. They told me to let it be, let it go, let it take its own course. I couldn't. When I heard they hadn't found a body I was sure I could get Rick out. I was ready to tear the jail down with my bare hands. But the lawyers told me I couldn't spring him because some old Indian saw it, and Rick's own brother. When they told me Pongo was ready to talk I laughed—He's never spoken a word in his life! And then I heard him. They played me a tape, said it was the boy, and even though

I've never heard him speak, couldn't possibly know how he would sound, I just knew that was his voice. It had to be. That crushed me, but the next time I went to the jail I got turned inside out even worse. I had never asked him, didn't want to know, but Rick told me—he didn't know why but he knew it was true, he stabbed that man who was looking for Pongo, stabbed him dead. <u>And you are that man</u>!

*   *   *

Rick is released. There is a celebration banquet at a very fancy restaurant. Red brings Kenneth. Rick is there with the two hookers, Monica and Sibel (who never speaks a word but "Whoopsie!"). They await Pongo (the boy) and Madge (Johnny Looking Cloud in a dress). The proprietor of the restaurant rounds out the party. Rick expresses convincingly his new purpose in life, to rebuild the Chilton Hotel, the wreck which is the last remnant of his father's inherited fortune.

The story culminates in these persons working with each other to rebuild and operate the Chilton Hotel. Monica and Kenneth develop an intimacy based entirely differently from either of their previous deviant adaptations (banker and prostitute, but I forget who had been which).

The boy speaks the final words, yelling up to the window where Monica and Kenneth have been sleeping:

<u>Pongo:</u> Hey, you two, wake up! It's been morning all day long. Madge says we've all worked hard enough this week, so we're all going to the mountain meadow for a picnic—and Red says he's going to teach me how to catch fish!

The final scene is a panorama of the mountains (which had previously been seen microscopically or as threateningly overlooming.)

*   *   *

A CONVERSATION BETWEEN A MAN AND A BOY

1. Unsure

Unsure how to begin this conversation, now realizing it is much older than he is, he feels older, much older than a moment ago. Techniques of communication seem complex when he has forgotten the meaning he seeks. It is important to remember this is a meaning he has once touched, but he has lost conscious cosmic rootedness.

He is convinced he smelled, tasted and knew meaning as a child. Every one must. By insisting to himself that *they* knew no better (the grownups then), he has allowed bitterness at the loss of animal senses to be ameliorated, transcending what he was taught. In other words, he was taught that big people knew the truth, and their knowledge gave them authority over him. Now he knows they know no better than what they do and how they do it, and they usually do it callously and blindly.

He knows no better himself, having brutalized his own children, having overpowered those about him, having brutalized, silenced and isolated his own child within. Now he intends to open negotiations with that child-self, to show good faith, to ask for help so that he can live.

Before I can ask for forgiveness I must forgive myself. My acceptance of the adults and authorities in my life (that they know no better) must be authentic, and it is that sort of forgiveness I must offer myself also. Before I can approach this heart of mine I have to forgive me, I have to accept the man I am and thereby accept all adult human beings in a manner kinder than I had imagined possible. It is not merely possible, but terrifyingly joyous.

And I must find my inner child, offer honestly what I can to him, hope he will not continue hating me. I need him desperately.

It is kind of you to come with me on an uncharted journey which is likely to be painful for me, dry and tedious for you. I do not know which way to go nor how we ought be provisioned. So, immediately come! I lead you with my unknowing.

2. It Is A Wood

It is a wood. I am not surprised. Anticipating a place severe and cold (but never prepared for the actuality of what hurts, what is severe or cold) I am relieved. I say "relieved," not "pleased," because to me it seems pleasure comes from what I am and what I do—to be pleased with myself—and placation comes from what you do for me, your attempts to please me (as if you ever could). Relief is more objective, more realistic—that I do not suffer the freezing and the beating which might have been forced on me.

It is a wood. I am relieved. The air is warm, even the shadows. The air is alive not with writhing teeming insects and fetid invisible mist of rotting biota, but modest and unveiled air gives out each of the discrete many extensions of this wood's beings. Even I can distinguish balsam, spruce, grasses' dust, flowers whose names I do not know, moss and mud and moistness of this shaded stream whose odors clearly sing to my nose exactly who it is, but no more clearly than its living self is sung to my ears by its gurgling kindly voice or even its relationship to me bespoken by the sound of my feet springily squishing at its water's edge (reinforced by the proprioception—my feeling of myself in my own parts—of my ankles' movements' waving minusculely on the gelid ocean of a foot wide band of mulch-covered mud) . . . and the vision! beings, shapes and movements, colors, change of colors—all coordinated with the sounds and smells, each of which itself has told the whole story, and altogether very much a symphony—but "symphony" means "sounds together" rather than "everything together here and now in all senses, named and unnamed"—and all together relating to me, because I also am here, and it is more amazing than magic that I also in this am a part and make smells in stirring air which I also stir, and can eat this all into my senses and live and be nourished, and as well and as happily I can recline here to be devoured by all that is about me (and ultimately I cannot decline so to be devoured) and I am actual, and all the more myself by being sensate.

It is a wood. Now that I have sensed it I sense it is familiar to me. Perhaps this is the sense of being home anywhere outdoors, away from cities where each alone we are always lost. Of being lost in the forest shall I believe contrived intimidating tales of terror and witchly and never-was-nor-never-will-be-monsterly consumptions of innocents? (Is it not the terrifying tale which destroys innocence?) I am sure there are real beings-lost in real forests, but even I have felt uncannily at home on a mountain, in a field, at the beach picking through the shells and rocks huge Ocean gives me as I weavingly dance in and out the edge of her surf whose waning froth caresses my feet and toes (dry, covered private parts of me usually, not moved, not shown, not shared) churning sand like fragrant steaming coffee grounds. The "part" of me which must succeed must never get lost, but the "part" of me which needs to live must be free to wander without fear of wandering. And if there is a "part" of me which wishes to survive . . . ?

I know where we are! Don't ask me how till later. Now follow me. We'll get along somehow. I feel it will be a long way and a long time before we are back where we recently were, maybe never, but what we must do now is to be here and move along without any guarantee of anything. Don't worry. I feel better about this every moment. Don't trust me; trust all of life. Thanks for being with me. I can't reciprocate in any concrete way, but I do thank you. Come.

3. Tree-Like

Come to a clearing abruptly as we have been making our way down the mountain between each pair of thick trees which stand close to each other respecting one the other all the way around. (Trees are not two-faced but all-faced, relating to the full sphere of their environs, not only through a horizon 360° about them but also into the air and the very sun, and into the earth and all nourishment, rootedness and grounding.) And now down we are at a mountain meadow, now out of the shadow, now standing in tall, stiff but giving grass at our legs, knees, even at our hips, brushing our perinea gently with broad red leaves and wheaty feather tips as we walk slowly, smiling beyond the frowning habit I have left to haunt the darker forest.

I have been here. I fear nothing although I know nothing. I do not remember a single detail or name, but I have some sense I have been here before . . . Yes! That must be it—I have some sense. For the first time in an immeasurable time I have some common sense. I have left the city and I have left society, which seems merely a struggle to invest energy and wrest value in return, pivots on competition, willingness to steal, willingness against all inner resistance to kill, and so my willingness to die. Away from the city, daring to move I feel entirely different, and I cannot master in ideas or capture in words all that is, so I rattle as if I could, as if I must . . . and I apologize for disturbing the air. I shall try to allow myself silence, rest my verbal armory and just be here with you tree-like.

4. Run

And sleeping in soft grass as if at home beside the dark stream's coherent murmurings has brought broad dreams of what is—stepping deer, their sounds in grass exactly as their thin legs are, narrow shafts whose points just touch the surface of Earth's face's great extent to indicate the distant deep reality of Center, deers' legs swishing timely, orderly through grass as if they were the raspy hairs of the violin bow sliding toward and away, sonating through the instrument which brain and muscle have made, the score which is modeled from All Life, and is noted in the genes; skitters of rodents underneath the leaves perhaps, producing rustles from far higher than their squat bodies reach; asynchronous splashes arising distinct from the water's constant silver tinkle and hollow gulping drum which may come from jumping fish or diving frogs or wading deer . . . or, for all I know, from gaily dancing stones. As I dream I hear each brilliant star—whose place and face and rhythm I have just now seen in the magnifying sky for the first ecstatic time—and each star has her simple song for me, a good night kiss.

And rested, truly rested, not cold as if deprived of warmth but cool, inert and firm, at one with the soft earth which molded to me, held me through this night. Without an agenda I do not know what is my energy. Waking here free I do not know how to act, but . . . D'you know? . . . I'm not afraid of acting bad. I'm not afraid of acting. I'm not afraid. I'm not aware of acting. I'm not acting. I am. I am aware. I am here. I am here with you. Now. Good morning, friend.

But there is something I must do. It is the reason we have come, of course. To find him. I must find him. Come. Run.

We make for ourselves difficult tasks and we have difficulty executing them. From my sense that this is the place to begin I drive myself to leave where I am, as if I must go in order ultimately to arrive. Even I know this is not being in the here and now with equanimity, but instead a doing of violence to what is true to me, crashing out into the world as if I would dig it all apart to find some great jewel. Another sterile myth on which to tear my flesh.

We crash across this meadow high in the air where we have rested and been grounded in the sky, downwards. Down our heaviness pulls us toward the greater heaviness of the flattening Center. I believe we are making progress as we go down the mountain, following the ever-growing stream. Run, Virgil.

5. Skittering Down The Scree

Skittering down the scree, squirrels in the trees chittering faster and faster, chasing each other mating, faster and faster we slide and skate downhill on small sharp rocks, huge innumerable boulders mirroring the mobile multitude of pebbles. If I am not in harmony with all nature, at least I am in harmony with gravity. I am elated to be traveling down the mountain faster than I can, and in my manic grandiosity I believe it cannot hurt you to be dragged by me, it cannot hurt me to hurtle down too fast to be overtaken by sluggish danger.

I have not completely forgotten my purpose here, but all I know of the boy is that I seek him, and all I know of the agenda is that I sensed I knew the high mountain meadow, that it stimulated my intuition to go down to the bottom to find him. I, the analyst, could not be wrong to follow my intuition. If it feels so right it can't be wrong.

All day I run and drag you. Without abating physically I dream waking, racing in my mind as in my legs. I know you are not Virgil in all truth, Publius Virgilius Maro whom Dante Aligheri fantasized to be his guide through hell. I know you are my silent friend whose presence has preserved me from isolated desperation. Most of the time I do not question your acceptance of me as I am, because I so much need it, but there are moments when my mind wavers and my heart quivers knowing there is nothing especially acceptable in me, nothing I give you, nothing for you to accept. But, thank you.

And I dream waking of the boy. Sweat pours, cakes my face. My legs and thighs ache to numbness but still are stiff enough each footfall to pound the rocky earth beneath me as if my pounding feet eventually will flatten all the earth. He is whom I see. What deep and empty eyes! He is distant from me now, and I fear when I come near him he will run, but he is the only thing I see, and I run to him, and I run, and run, run.

6. Necessity

Through the mountain woods all day we have run beside the swelling river in and out of demarcated territories, bank and wood. Now somewhere beyond the exhaustion which has chased me I collapse at the edge of the mountains, the edge of the flatlands, on these foothills barren of calm old trees, on these foothills sparsely vegetated by brush and grasses.

Necessity is with us now. My being exhausted doesn't take away the need to eat, but redoubles it. It will be dark, and soon the simplest provision for our needs will be beyond us. Now I scramble for wood, and not later. Now I gather grass for us to sleep in. Now you fetch water from the river to boil for drinking. Now you boil the beans.

Could it be the weather changed? Is it only because the sun has left us, or is it the change in altitude, the winds? The trees . . . they protected us before, I think, and now we are beyond them. This is what once was the beach of the inner ocean, all before us huge blue sea. Now it is the flatness of its bottom, grass growing and highways into nowhere. It is colder and darker now than I wish to suffer, and it is not yet quite night, and it is not yet even into fall.

We huddle into a depression, covered over and under by grass wrapped in our ponchos. Wind rushes to us like a big pet dog might rush from the cold pond shaking water to soak and freeze me when I was a child too small to run or authoritatively bark "No!"; or like a black sleek cat it brings to us, like to the doorway a dead rat, dense disorienting dark. To walk on these burning numb worn legs is near impossible now, and through my cavelike blindness I cannot help but reel and fall on this inclined plain. This is not the ancient beach, I swear, but as I lurch and curse and fear I'll drown I know this is the ancient ocean raging.

There is no sleeping, nor any warmth in huddling together. There is no dreaming, just the delirium of pain. My head rolls in pain and my face throbs with burning ice inside my sinuses. My frustrated tears scream blame at everything about me. I can see nothing in this dark, but if it were midday could see nothing, eyes clamped shut in pain. Pain exists only as a reality, either is or isn't, either on or off—at least this is what I believe as I writhe and wish for the serenity I think is death to turn off absolutely either the nauseating headache or my life.

If the warning itself can kill me, what further peril do I risk to go to the very bowels of hell? Last morning I was comfortable and thrilled with the out of doors. Now I am so pained I fear I can't continue, and therefore I do. Because it can't be done I must do it. I am resolved to persevere, spend the interminable night in anger. Dawn's fingers tickle me. I have energy again to drag you far beyond the gates of hell. For no reason my pain is gone, and for all my purposes my anger drives me—anger unafraid and raging, indefatigable anger.

7. In Ways No Animal Will

Down the hill, still along the unstill river whose waters are red from isotopes of iron it has ingested at this place of ancient cataclysm where the earth's face was thrust up and the lowest solid levels of its crust came to jut vertical like rocket ships poised to shoot the stars. Iron tinges the water red and I call it bloody.

We march over expanses of flattening grassy desert devoid of surprises. When we were in the mountains distant yesterday we could not see before us but a step or ten and every step promised every thing good and bad—from behind every rock a monster or a maiden, at every little clearing a unicorn or a behemoth, around each bend a castle or a conflagration; and now pale miles extend calm and unexciting, promising nothing but more marching step upon step upon step. Yesterday was an unreal respite in the tedious unmoving flow of my existence, for yesterday was filled with new space, new time, new being and high purpose—my energy came from being alive—and today again is extensive tedium through which I march tired and pained, energized by unrelenting fury which is the mindless refusal to die.

Or is it so desolate? A small black clot on the prairie before us. I cannot know what it is, and you, my friend, avoid knowing anything. So, marching apace we approach it slowly, and the "it" becomes a "them" as I watch figures moving in ways no animal will: all dark, and almost indiscernible at this distance; many stationary at their center but some orbiting about the clump like bees, and some speeding in and out the periphery spewing clouds of dust, glinting sparkles which penetrate the dark and darkening sky.

I had forgotten time and space and cultural distance throughout my moment on the mountain, so I am surprised to see something from my own culture, place and time—bikers. I suppose I still wish unicorns and fairies. There are at least a hundred here, and more coming up the highway I now see, in droves or herds or gams or globs (or whatever you will call a group of motorcycles)—no one alone. I look for Hunter S. Thompson (someone my own age) as if to see him actually would make a sight gag for myself, all in my own head—and there he is! slung over a keg, an important writer, an unimportant drinker.

Jimmy is the one who greets us, chosen by authority of silent fate as anarchy here raucously refuses to reign. He is short, thick, belligerent and warmly welcoming, staunch in his black leather, somewhat hunched from adapting his body away from recently learned erectness halfway back to belly-crawling, the conformation which leans the torso almost horizontal, arms extended, to ride and mate with machine and monster Harley Davidson. His gold tooth glints beneath a gold and grey handlebar mustache almost bigger than his face. Head bandanna-bound and one gold earring give him the pirate look. (I look for the hook, but see two hands tattooed with birds and snakes, all nine fingernails dyed in dirt and oil.)

> "Beer! Beer! Get these pilgrims some beer!"

> "No, thanks, Jimmy. I don't drink any more."

> "Grass! We have plenty of grass. Get these mendicants some weed!"

> "No, thanks, Jimmy. I don't smoke marijuana either."

"Well, you can't have any of our girls. And don't try."

"How about a place to rest a bit. We have been walking hard and hurt and cold. May we stop here for a while?"

"Who's stopping you?"

8. An Old Purse

Again I cannot sleep. More images rage, pointing me to something, I believe. It is not the noise of the chaos about me, but that which is within me which turns me inside out like an old purse, empties me onto the table, half spilled on the floor, to see what I have, only to find a profusion of meaninglessness, the equivalents of worn illegible receipts, chewed gum, small change, depleted tubes of make-up, seventeen lipsticks, Binaca, shreds of tobacco, an address book, Binaca, sunglasses with one ear piece, a Harlequin romance, wrinkled photographs, Binaca, a billfold without money, a scissor whose points are broken off, Binaca, little scissor points, breath mints . . . and what fell to the floor can bloody well stay there until someone else comes by to pick them up each little bit and put them in his purse and carry them about meaningless, like Jimmy.

9. Conversation With A Stranger

And dark comes, and fires give cold light. Despite the noise and whirling dancing, despite the screams of drunken warriors and thrilled and frightened women, despite the singing and the several radios, guitars, and even a harmonica, despite the crash of fist fights, thuds of bodies against sides of vans and hoods of cars, despite the crickets in the grassy plain I am mercifully relieved of hearing what is outside about me, know only murky repeated themes within me which point collapsed me to inflate myself and sail further down, to the very bottom of the ocean, off these shoals and into the deep, to find the boy, to find me.

Despite my drivenness I am exhausted—but what is the end of energy? Even beyond death, whatever that may be, I expect someone or something to take the stuff of me into its belly to fuel it into some further beyond. I could go now, but I know it contradicts common sense to move before morning, and I know I owe you a chance to rest a bit before I drag you farther.

There is nothing glamorous about a drunk biker, nor about a drunk ballerina either. Each was there in numbers, becoming numb. Jimmy, having roared his bike, having sung his songs, having slapped backs and punched arms comes to sit calmly, seems interested to enter conversation with a stranger (to exit that conversation with a friend).

"Why you traveling this way?"

"This way? You mean in this fashion or in this direction?"

16

"Both the How and the Tao."

"Wow! You would appear to be a criminal drunken devilish wild man, and you make subtle discriminations. And you are not drunk, despite appearances."

"I don't drink any more."

"And do you drink any less? Thereby hangs a tale."

"You know my story. Maybe not the details, but the meat."

"How do you get here?"

"By my bike. And where do you think you're going?"

"You know my agenda. Maybe not the details, but the mashed potatoes."

"You are looking for yourself and the deeper you go the loster you get. You seem frantic trying to master the mountain. You seem frightened trying to meet people. You have some idea of what you want to do, but you don't understand you can't do it. It must be done *for* you, and that will come when you are ready, and it won't be what you have planned."

"Can I trust you?"

"Can you? Who is more trustworthy than a stranger? How can I harm you, other than to kill you? I certainly won't gossip about you, 'cause I don't care about you. And you have no reason to care what I think of you, do you?"

"No, I suppose I don't. But if you don't care and if I don't care, why do I want to tell you about me, and why are you willing to hear me?"

"Because I have been heard, and now I can hear again. Being heard won't fix you, but go ahead, I'm listening."

As I tell him my story I hear some of it too. Deprivation, violence, threats, rejection, isolation, shame, hidden impossible expectations, sexual exploitation, loss, grief, conflict, competition, anger, guilt, depression—all repeated themes in the story of a fairly normal person. I wonder how much more lurid will be the story of such an outlaw as Jimmy. And sudden insight lets me understand it is the same. We remember experiences because we perceive them. If we could perceive other levels of the reality about and within us, we would experience and remember those. I don't hear the dog whistle, so I don't respond to or remember it, but the dog does. And my dog is puzzled at my responses, no doubt. So, because we humans are vulnerable to our own spectrum of emotions, we remember the experiences which stimulated those emotions as our own stories. We all remember through our tears, our fears and pains and angers, not through any "objective reality" in the world. And so our stories are the same, but we cannot remember them but poorly because we forget, hoping, perhaps, to evade pain; and we become less sensitive, numbed in our armor. It is just so simple, but saying it doesn't fix it. I have to live it. Now I know I must be open to everything, vulnerable, in order to find what I wish or need. I must be ready and willing, but I need not be able to do anything but ask for help.

10. Calmer

Calmer this morning, ready to walk, but not so interested in going anywhere. Just walk. We rest often, and I tell you of my conversation with Jimmy. You seem as bland about my insights as you seem about my fury, you infuriating Buddha! If I didn't know you cared about me I would walk off without you or kill you and throw your body in the ditch beside the highway. You show no emotion, but you are so sensitive. Listen to me!—I answered my own question: You show no emotion (but that's not completely true—you smile blissfully when you pray), and you consciously feel your own feelings.

The highway is an easy path to walk, still downhill, still not on the level. Not many cars come by, but those speeding. I judge my progress not in terms of them, but as my own tired legs, my own sore feet and my happy ears hearing my own unheard of whistling.

More cars, slower; more walking, on the level, no hurry. Now I recognize where we are with a very different part of my brain than that which felt the familiarity of the mountain and the meadow. My memory may be imperfect, but I know almost everything about the city we approach, where I spent my childhood, where my mother spent her childhood (and struggled never to leave). We could wave down a car and get a ride, but there is no need to do so. It is chilly, but not unbearable, so we walk on knowing we will sleep in a field or barn tonight instead of a hotel.

11. Float Or Fly

Mice, but, finally, rest. A barn might have been more comfortable, but here we are. This motel was never glamorous, but now why is it? Why does it exist? Why isn't it something else, or somewhere else or nothing? We are the only guests here, I am sure. We may be the only guests this month, this year.

I can see the city exactly as it was. No detail evades me as my mind travels the reality of my fantasy. From within my child bed in the house in which I lived I uncover myself abruptly, feet meet the floor, record the textures, temperatures and even colors of the rug I step on, the bare wood and the cold white bathroom tile. I haven't known what age I am until I find I must stand on tiptoe to pee over the edge of the toilet. And down the stairs and out. And freer now than at that age to go as far as I can go down the street of big old houses, many now subdivided into apartments, up the hill to downtown where big brick buildings loom so high and close together there is but a remnant of the sky flowing like a narrow banner straight above me flapping. Without effort I float or fly at good old ground level through each street which leads me south a mile or more to immense Swan Lake, almost a block across and more than a block along, where there are some swans in fact, but immensely many more ducks by hundreds, whose honking begging throng demand more bread. And easily to the end of town, a wood where rabbits thrive and machines and men today intend to build a shopping center so tomorrow rabbits will be gone to unimaginable nowhere and cars will park. Without effort I float or fly at scary sky level to the river, unpredictable mother of all joy and terror who predictably floods each spring and each fall, and between floods unpredictably except in summer when she predictably evaporates into a tiny thick black stream whom I could jump across except I am afraid because I have been told the quicksand will swallow me away. Flowing also along the river's side and equally unnavigable are the interwoven forest and thick brush of riverbank, and within and between them jump and swim the monsters of my world: snakes and rats and monstrous catfish, foot-round snapping turtles, bats.

Since it takes no real time or real effort I swing again about the city, slowly. Now persons are no blur. I see them, but I know I shall not touch them. Aesthenic neighbor Alice maintaining her garden in a bonnet, always at home while her husband is away for months at a time changing the world. Dicky Wheeler tormenting younger children, and dogs if he can get away with it. From this distance he is not so infuriating as pitiable. Madame Monett who cares for epileptics for a little money in the house she used to keep as the center of the city's social court when she was much younger and someone cared for opera. Rosemary fat, round pimple-faced gum-chewing unexcited cashier at the little movie house where watching serials and westerns with ten cent popcorn we were often the only customers in a day, a week. I do not know if she has a life, refuse to guess. Mario, a businessman, who soled shoes in his shop, but gradually bought the building and the block, expanded his shop and sold shoes. He knows my name, and I am just a kid; either he cares for kids and people or he courts customers early, or both. Coach Curly, who is bald, will try to intimidate me in junior high school by threatening to paddle me if I should misbehave, will become my friend because, I think, I will not be physically intimidated by him nor he intellectually intimidated by me. Josh, the driver of the only cab in town, parked at the same curb, chewing the same cigar, reading the same newspaper. The Coney Island where hot dogs have just gone up to eight cents apiece (but that includes everything—onions, mustard, kraut, relish and chili) where the young Greeks yell loudly in Greek, but the old man with warts on his face stolidly herds tame hot dogs on the grill for years and for forever absolutely silently in Greek.

And on? There are a hundred thousand persons here. Have I convinced you, or suggested even, that even self-preoccupied I can attend to other persons, who they are, what they wish and need? You, isolated Buddha who sees all silently; you, articulate Virgil who will not speak imperfectly in this imperfect world; you, sadistic angel from Heaven, inscrutable hindoo, Pancho Sanza—Wake up! Up and out with us! To the city, now. Let us go, you lumpy werewolf! Feet to the floor!

12. Recapitulate

I walk. I recapitulate, but cannot recapitulate, cannot remember clearly even yesterday. What I carry with me of yesterday is not yesterday but what I carry with me now. I know this moment walking what yesterday I dreamed waking, that I have left whatever life I had (which was killing me) to find the boy. I sensed him as soon as I was quite high on the mountain, but I have been driven to find him as far down as I can go in the city. I have a strong sense that he needs me, and even though I have taught me to need nothing, I have a strong need to sense him, who I used to be, who I will become.

Incredible! "Avalon, Population 1,000,000, Elevation Zero" Only the name has not been changed. Even the altitude has sunk! Whooda thunk? How can we be at the city when we haven't even reached the river? Where are we, really? Come, comrade.

Here are sterile flat avenues laid out with a straight edge. Everything is rectilinear and horizontal. Nothing distorts the checkerboard. It is impossibly more orderly than were the exact checkerboards of fields which were here when I was last here, but now they crawl with cars, all Japanese silver. There is not a face visible, not one. I stand at this moment at this intersection of streets, and if I censor out the moving cars, and if I pretend the meanings of the signs are Japanese beyond my understanding, then there is nothing moving or meaningful here, no life, no growth, no humanness. These fields are empty checkered expanses of miles, nothing growing. We move on.

Is this my river? I see before me a placid pond whose banks are no wilderness but a manicured park with cement walks and cement tables, benches. Could a child fly in this park a cement kite with a cement tail? Her waters used to wane and flow in powerful hormonal rhythm. This placid fullness is the product of a dam, like the horse's tail was part of what moved and flailed flies, danced (carrying with it as a dancing partner the whole horse, even a rider) by its own or some other power beyond you and beyond the city council, but is not at all the same when it has become a pillow stuffed with horse hair, puffy, sedate upon a sofa. And these pond and park are nothing like a river and its bank for engendering and nourishing monsters boys can love to fear or catch or listen to in the night rattling and rasping.

Thank God I am a man and not a boy, or I would be more than deeply disappointed. As a man I am capable of accepting these changes not only, but also am capable of originating and executing them. I can work hard and I can oppose my fellows to create what is sterile. I am the abortion.

The man can see this and walk on. I walk on, toward the center of the city. Rounding the only nonrectilinear structure in the county, a bend in the river, we see the center—tall buildings clumped in the middle of the plain, a circle three miles across rising out of the checkered flatness of the five miles each way surround, an elevation, a rising not unlike a large painful carbuncle pointing to a head. (Another time, another attitude I might call this the glorious citadel of Avalon, each structure a castle or cathedral, but I am subject to such romantic fantasies no longer.)

Walking these streets toward the center of the city we two holy pilgrims seem not to be seen to glow, but can feel silent stares reflect back to us our images as bums, butts of derision from behind tinted glass. Everything and everyone at street level is enclosed behind glass, either cars or storefronts. We are the only ones exposed. I am a man; I can persevere against derision by my own strength. Despite drastic changes in the face of my town I recognize the names of streets toward the center, and I sense the configuration, even, of blocks and buildings though it seems no building stands which was here then. I sense the configuration of where people lived and worked who now are gone. Reality remains like a ghost.

We reach the tall buildings and are not intimidated. We know what is sky, have read true sky and listened to the songs of stars. Eclipse by mere buildings is not blindness nor silence. We walk the blocks bounded by buildings which extend many dozens of yards above the ground and are called skyscrapers. These blinders bring our focus to the streets in which we see the figures of persons, and such persons we have never seen in just this way.

Tired evening in the city, whatever daylight traffic having waned, and we see leaving brightly shining costumes of pale and frantic persons clacking to their cars who flee the city to the suburbs, carrying paraphernalia manifold—brief cases, umbrellas, lunch boxes, gym bags, silver thermoses, personal computers, packages from shopping, cases of beer. It leaves us with those who live here emerging from the crannies, from basements, alleys, beneath loading docks and bridges. They are not brightly colored, but are colorful, full of the colors of disease (jaundice, pallor, rubor, just plain dirt from outside and from deep within the pores) and the color of being alive, imperfect—like the struggle to be honest in a tough and selfish world, and the struggle to remember who you are when no one else cares. Yes, now I see a difference between those brightly clad perfectly groomed yuppies who seek the preservation of the pretension of perfection, and those self-admittedly imperfect who may lie and steal but without pretension honestly admit unhesitatingly that they are merely human.

13. The Center

Is this the Center I sought? Is this where gravity leads me? I have felt driven, sometimes pained, frequently calmer than I have ever been, but always energized. I hadn't realized how empty my life had become during the creeping decades, how immediately I could be transported out and away from every thing about me which I could call "mine." Divested of possessions and obligations I haven't the slightest idea who I am, but I am immensely more self-possessed. I believe I wish to live, and if it were all over right now I will have lived, utterly unknowing but feeling I am whoever I am.

And this? Is this the center I sought, this flat and ordinary town of flat and ordinary people? Even I can see their individual faults and their communal catastrophes. I try not to hate them for all that, but I thought I was going somewhere at last, and this certainly seems nowhere. Having felt alive, I feel the deflation of having been cheated, as if I had been used.

And the sun sets on this dust-colorless city evening, and color and light creep out of the seeping sewers to the sterile streets and populate them with all the usual unique characters—the pimps, the hookers, the drunks and the junkies, the hustlers, the snitches, the hoboes, the johns, the waifs, the narcs, the prowlers, the loonies, the staggerers, the sleepers, the wanderers, the leerers and lookers, the bookies, a preacher, the dope peddlers of various sorts and shakes, the wolves, the snakes, the grandmothers who were too poor or demented to move from this wilderness carefully scuttling to safety they cannot have, the bikers, the skinheads, pale children in black, shopkeepers, sidewalk sweepers, two alien pilgrims, the parents cruising to find their runaways, the cops, squad car strobes in red and blue and white, and neon colored worms which signify succinctly, rather than to obfuscate expensively all practical meaning. A few contrasting examples suffice: "EATS", "CHECKS CASHED", "KEG LIQUORS"; "DEVIL'S DEN"; or will you prefer fancy daytime messages: "RAMBLE, SCRAMBLE, BIDIEUX AND WATTNIT, ATTORNEYS AT LAW"; "UNIBANK (A Division of Ultranational Financial, Ltd.)"; "FANDANGO BOUTIQUE"; "EUROPEAN SPECIALTY COMPANY"; "JOSE O'SHEA'S CONTINENTAL AND NOUVEAU-AMERICAN CUISINE"? Which sort of message tells you what is what? Which reveals and which obscures? Maybe there is an honesty for me here, but I am uncomfortable with it. The center of the city at night is a real time and a real place for me to be, but I don't like it. Now I remember something he wrote me years ago when I was more receptive, like an impossible postcard from a universe other than the one I came to inhabit:

Avalon
1950

My dear difficult and distant man,

I wish you knew what I go through. I wander down the streets. This town is dead despite the red and blue and white bright flashing light and noise from bars and whistles. Cars honk screeching, crash. It's all a flash, a blare, a gong. It's also wrong. It's also dead. Without a head a body's twitch (a city's twitch) awaits the last long gasp (foul blast from a gurgling gash). A heave, a crash, and all to hell a city fell alive with a million screaming maggots.

Yours, truly,
Pongo Bernoulli
(not my real name)

14. The Carnival

I know he can't be here, but this is where I have been drawn. I don't want to find him here, but I really do want to find him. What next? Whatever is before me, of course. So who could help, who could know . . . ? I know that man! See him walking, across the street, the one in the hunter's jacket?

"Hey, Red! Don't run away from me. I'm not a cop. I just want you to help me with something important to me. It won't take long. Wait up."

"Hey, man, I'm really busy, so . . ."

"I'm looking for a boy . . ."

"That's not unusual. There are plenty on this street . . . See? Three standing on this very block, right in plain sight, cheap."

"No, you don't understand. I'm looking for a special boy. Can we talk for a few minutes?"

"Can I talk you into buying me a drink in a few minutes?"

"Sure. Anything you say."

"The Carnival, next block. I'll be there in ten minutes. Right now I gotta do something, bad. Won't be long. Back booth. It'll be open. It's mine."

We wait where ten minutes is a long time if you're not drinking. Usual smells—beer and piss and cigarettes, bad cigarettes, shaggy old Bugler, wet butts. Usual unique characters—baggy old dirty work clothes, unshaven but no beards cultivated, nursing beers mostly quiet, eruptions of laughter or anger every few minutes brief, jukebox and television fights not really in competition because even though each is loud no one listens to either. We wait, and I am not used to waiting. We wait, and in a short ten minutes I learn the valuable lesson that ten minutes can be a long time for me to wait.

"Okay. I'm fixed. Whatcha want?"

"I'm looking for a boy . . ."

"Dj'you ferget my drink? I did'n. My brain works better'n yours."

I don't know how I know Red. Perhaps I drank with him. He certainly resembles Hunter S. Thompson. He finally settles in the booth across from me, beer in one hand, Wild Turkey in the other (double shot). He certainly resembles Hunter S. Thompson.

"My brain works better when I have something to hold onto with each hand—keeps me from fidgeting, concentrate better. Now, tell ol' Red the problem. I always understand. I've seen everything, done everything."

"I'm looking for a special boy. I don't know exactly how old. I don't know how to describe him. I only know I need to find him . . ."

"I understand. It's easy. See Rick at the Devil's Den. He's his pimp. He'll get you together with him. It won't be cheap, but it will be worth it for you."

"You don't understand. I'm looking for a certain special boy. I think he's somewhere around here. I'm not looking for . . ."

"We're all looking for something, and heaven help us if we find it. Everyone's looking for something except me. Whatever it is, I've already had it. That's how come I understand everything, and I understand what you want, and I told you how to get it, and if you want it start at the Devil's Den, and if you don't bring me another drink."

"And that's all?"

"Yep . . . Nope, bring me another drink anyhow. And get your ass to the Devil's Den and find Rick and find the boy and pay for it and get what you want . . . and get me another drink."

"I don't think you understand what I'm looking for, that I'm . . ."

"Nope? Yep, I do. And I understand you don't trust even me, and you're the one who came to me for advice. Well, here's my advice—get me another drink and get going."

15. Curiouser And Curiouser

I'm beginning to feel like Alice. The world is getting curiouser and curiouser, and everything around me is getting ridiculous. Is "the Devil's Den" a daytime disinforming denotation, or an earthy truth of the city sewer? I have enough difficulty beginning to know my own sensations and ideas without having to tangle with convoluted meanings in the world around me. How can I afford to follow any suggestions whose outcomes I cannot anticipate? I have been willing enough to follow my own impulses when they feel right, but how can I do what Red says—even though it was my impulse to ask him—when I feel he doesn't understand me, and when I don't understand how it can work out . . . but I said I would wander where each step took me, each moment, and it may be more important to follow my program than to stay safe, and even if the people around me misunderstand or have invalid purposes and even if I don't know how I feel and even if I don't understand what's happening and even if I can't guess the outcome I can keep my integrity by honestly being who I am, even with my doubts and my unknowing, and when I make my faux pas I can dance another direction the next moment because I am free now . . .

Hey, pal, here's a song I make for you. (You didn't know I had verbal capacities of an artistic sort?):

> Thanks
> not for this day
> but for this moment.
> Mobile I
> through this city

of fixed old buildings,
mobile biped
slow but upright mostly,
knowing walking
is falling forward
and daring to take a step,
pick up a foot and place it
before me,
and not just either foot
but the one which was behind,
and knowing dancing also
is falling
one way,
then another,
and there are innumerable dimensions
even in the city
in which to fall
and from which to recover.
And thanks
that I am not alone here,
but others are pedestrian upright.

Hello.
Will you care to dance with me?

I mean it. Thanks for being with me in this moment of madness.
Come. Dance! Let me spin you till you're dizzy. Trust me. I won't
let you fall. Move your feet fast. Tap. Shuffle. I love it! I can move!

I collapse on the curb, feel the heat rush through me, the sweat
erupt in its moment, flow hot then cool. I know most all of me
is here now. Perhaps to be me is more than to have merely
sensations and images, but to be moving and panting, to dare
to dance. And thank me for being with me in this moment of
sanity.

And now to the Devil's Den. I'm ready for what it is.

16. The Devil's Den

Although it is only blocks away we pass its obscure portal three times before we recognize to enter it. Down narrow steps and down, farther than I thought the digging of a building's basements would be allowed (although I know mines are excavated miles beneath the surface, and so should know it can be done). Only slightly aware of my own thoughts I wonder what it is all about, what it is like, and skim my shallow fantasy that the Devil's Den is Hades, and although I absolutely do not entertain belief in hell (nor does belief in hell entertain me at all) I have dull images of hellish stereotypes so common I consider they debase all other clichés (to which I attribute some ringing-true lest they would not have become clichés). And my fantasies do not prepare me to accept what it is, whatever it is.

It is a dive. The Devil's Den is bleak and not at all colorful. The red and blue bulbs cast so little light they leave the eye straining to discern forms dark and colorless. Oh, you can make out everything, but no detail or inherent hue is manifest. It is as if your eyes felt things blindly in the dark, like radar outlining the somethings, where they are, but not at all like it would be to see a streaking screaming silver fighter plane spinning and careening, laying out its spider-web fiber staid and stable in the sky as the plane itself is mercurialness, this cloudy trail a flag, a battle banner strong but flexible in the wind left behind by its airplane-lover in his wake so that even were the plane to crash this flag would remain waving like a delicate white woman with a white lace handkerchief, would still stand on the platform loyal when the train had long gone from sight—but here is none of the shape and color and detail and character which would be in the white sky of bright day—just blips, the scantiest pattern only, by which a submarine carefully will navigate the profoundest blackest depths perilous and oppressive.

It is a pit. Speakers scream molten heavy metal, but the energy of the music has no effect on the deathly dark of several dozen inert faces pasted to the stools and in the corners of the booths. I wonder how I will find Rick. (I do not wish to ask or in any way reveal myself.) I want to leave, to go back . . . but back to what? I suppose I could return to where I was, the apartment, the job, the emptiness I insisted was okay with me . . . but why? All I have is to move on in front of me, to find him, to find my own beyond now. And here and now is the Devil's Den, and there is nothing I want here, only what I need. How can I find Rick?

17. Monica

"Looking for someone, good looking?"

"Huh?"

"I'm Monica. Come sit with me. Come. Right here on the stool next to me so I can look at you."

"Oh, okay. I just happened in, just came to look around."

"Until you saw me."

"Until I saw you, and came to sit with you."

"Buy me a drink."

"Okay, I'll but you a drink, but I don't want you to misunderstand. I have an important errand. I really don't have time to visit."

"Oh, so you think I'm only interested in one thing. Well, I'm not. I'll be glad just to visit for a while, so make yourself at home. Do you think I'm beautiful?"

I could see Monica was beautiful even before I could see anything else in this crowded darkness. Now all I can see is more of her beauty. But why such beauty in a whore? I do not blame her for how she is, but why. She is white, all white. She is long and pale, her dress is white eyelet taffeta puffed at he shoulders and dipped at the breast (and her breasts are pale as marshmallows as I see and almost smell the warm dry softness of their sugar powder surface when she dips to pick up her carefully dropped handkerchief), her hair is silver white, and in her hand she holds the white lace handkerchief which sketches vapor trails in the dark as she freely gesticulates pointing to herself, opening her arms away into the distant sky, and again pointing to herself.

"Oh yes, you are beautiful, Monica."

"You're not so bad yourself. What is this terrible errand you must do, rather than to spend some time with me?"

"No one seems to understand, and I am beginning to understand why. I am looking for a boy I hope is here. I have come to feel incomplete without him, but the only way I know to look to find him is to follow my intuitive impulses. I am a very practical and rational man—at least I was—and I don't understand what I am doing, but I must do it. Does that make any sense to you?"

"No. But don't let that worry you, honey. You just go find that boy. And if you ever get it straight and have enough time—and money—come see me."

"I understand that you don't understand, but that will have to be okay. Here's twenty for the drink (I hope you get part of it), and twenty for you if you will answer a question for me: How can I find Rick?"

Cold white shoulder.

18. Rick

Rick finds me. I have never seen someone appear young and innocent in every detail, and over all evil. Maybe it's the snakeskin boots that seem so evil, but the large-lensed spectacles and broad cheeks and smile seem open and friendly; maybe his modest unflamboyant garb is unthreatening, but somehow the suggestion of a ducktail in his combed back short curls latently signifies his narcissism. Over all he's evil in the manner anyone is who is ready to offer you something, but for his own sake. Beware Greeks bearing gifts, but don't look a gift horse in the mouth.

"Howdy, stranger. You lookin' for somethin'?"

"I'm looking for Rick."

"You found him."

"I felt so. I'm not surprised."

"Who sent you to me, Partner?"

"Red."

"Sure. He's an old reliable. You can count on Red; he won't steer you wrong. So, what can I do you out of today?"

"It's tonight, and I'm looking for a boy . . ."

"No problem."

". . . a very special boy."

"Absolutely."

"I don't know what name he goes by or how old he is—even approximately—or what he looks like, but . . ."

"No problem. Keep talking; I'm getting an idea what you need. Keep talking, buddy. You seem a little nervous. No need to be. Whatever it is you want in a boy—or in a girl—or in a boy and a girl—I can get it for you 'wholesale', if you get my drift. Any friend of Red's is a friend of mine, and nothing is too good for my friends."

"I thought Red didn't understand what I mean, and I think you don't understand what I mean, and I thought I wanted to be understood, but maybe I'm learning to tolerate being misunderstood, and maybe I'm learning to let things go the way they go and to go along with them . . . So, what do you recommend, Rick?"

"It won't be cheap, but it will be well worth it. Ah gay-ron-tee."

"How much?

"Two-five-oh. Two hundred and fifty dollars."

"Where and when?"

"Chilton Hotel, twenty minutes. Meet me in the lobby, pay me there. Cash, no checks or credit cards—not in this particular trade."

Of course none of this can come out straight, but halfway down the winding yellow brick road I'm not likely to find a vacant taxi.

19. The Chilton

Never was the Chilton elegant. I have seen many old hotels, and even through the glum dust on the twelfth level of waterstained peeling faded truly ugly geometric untruly patterned wallpaper, and through the layers of white and brown and green and brown and white and brown and white and runny off-white thick globbed paint on the surviving balusters which might even have been turned by hand, and even through the clutter of the small lobby now overstuffed with ragged overstuffed furniture and too many end tables and coffee tables and a black and white television and magazine racks, and even through what often is candid squalor I can see the elegance someone once intended for a hotel. But not the Chilton—no hidden nor dead elegance here. None.

It's not really a lobby, just a stairwell with a table. This is not the place I wish to wait. Let's go out on the street. Rick will likely see us outside the door.

I hate waiting. I am not programmed for it. If I stop being busy nothing good can happen, only nothing (and that's not good) or something bad. I suppose I'm afraid if I stop I'll just stop. I suppose I'm afraid I'll die. Where is he? It has been more than twenty minutes, more than thirty. I miss my watch. I came along this journey unprepared. I brought nothing but myself. You are the one who has come up with the necessities. I could have provided for us if I had had the time. You always know what I need. What's this? Thanks. Two-hundred-fifty exactly.

Where is he? It has been more than thirty minutes, I am sure. I can't wait to see him, although I know this can't be the one I'm looking for, not under these conditions, not a pimp directing me to him as if he were a prostitute. None the less, I have a vivid image of climbing those splintered old creaky stairs, opening a dingy door seeing him seeing me back, hesitating a moment to take it in, and running to embrace each other. Again I feel closer to what drives me to him. We need each other. I can't wait to see him.

It has been thirty-two minutes, at least. Where is Rick? I know he would be gone if he had gotten any money, but he hasn't. He couldn't have come by us. I hate waiting. I can't wait to see the boy. I have to wait to see the boy. I have to wait. I can wait. I don't like waiting. How can you wait so calmly? What do you think during the minutes, the hours. Are you stupid and empty?—I'm sorry for having said that. I know you are most sensitive and insightful. I also know I need not apologize, that your feelings are not likely to be hurt by anything I say.

Where is Rick? It seems like hours. I haven't seen anything of him up or down the street. Have you? I think of the boy, wonder why I need him so much, wonder what all this means, remember I was at the end of my existential rope, felt the need to know him, to hold him, to be loved by him. Now I wish my hope were stronger, my image clearer. I feel if I could focus, meditate on this one most important aspect of my life's whole history for an interminable timeless moment, find calm in the silence of the wordless meaning of this delicate hidden aspect of my self in the aura of the soft power in which all else gently fades into unimportance . . .

> "Where have you been? I've been waiting for you for thirty minutes. I looked in the lobby a dozen times."

> "We've been standing here waiting for you. How did you get past us?"

"I came through the back door. Are you sure you want to do this?"

"Yes, more than ever, and if I don't make it this time, then it will be the next one or the next one, but I will find the boy."

"Do you have the money? I'll take it now, and I will be right in front of you until I leave you with him. Understand now, nothing funny with this boy. He's special. Pongo is mute, has never said a word . . ."

"Did you say 'Pongo'?"

"Yeah. That's not his real name, but that's what we've called him ever since I can remember. You seem interested in something besides having a little fun with him."

"I am."

"Well, then I'll tell you the truth. He is a boy, I swear, and that's all people who want a boy need to know. But he's 'legal', that is prostitution isn't exactly 'legal' around here, but me and my dad don't like dealing with little kids, I mean like twelve-year-olds like some guys on the street handle. I don't think we've ever employed anyone under sixteen, and hell, that's adult enough, don't you think? But don't get me wrong, Pongo is a little boy, just like you want, but . . . Look, it's kinda unusual, but it's all okay, and this is a little boy, but he'll do everything you want him to, but in years he isn't so young. Look, I don't know why I'm telling you this, but I'll try to tell the rest. I'm not used to telling the truth, and sometimes it gets by me, but I don't know what it is about you that makes me want to tell you all this, and you're probably not interested, so if you want to just forget the whole thing I'll do something I've never

done before, honestly . . . Here's you money back right
now, if you want it."

"No, not at all. Never. You keep the money. Please
take me to the boy. But first, and before you lose your
delicate train of truth, finish what you were telling me.
I really care."

"Well, I guess things are alright, after all. And you're
alright too."

"Thanks. And you're all right, too."

"Follow me, and I'll tell you as we go. We have a bit of
walking to do. Only the first two flights are these creaky
old hotel steps. Most of the way down are steps carved
in the rock. Don't fall on me—it's dark and narrow, but
I know the way, and it's not as difficult as it seems.
You wanted to know the true story about the kid? Well,
about twenty years ago my dad was still in this trade
and he come across this kid who had been found tied
to a radiator and he didn't talk and his eyes was spacy
and his face and arms was a little hairy (but not like he
had a beard or anything) and he was just like putty,
that is he would do anything you said. We took him to
the doctor to see if he was sick, and the doctor said
he was okay, but sometimes deaf or severely abused
kids are just like that, mute and a little hairy. But he's
not deaf, because he will come or do things when
I tell him, without reading my lips, like from the next
room. For a long time Pongo was at our place, kinda
like a dumb little brother when I was growing up. Then
when Red would go around on business Pongo and
me would go with him, and when Pongo saw what
prostitutes do he wanted to do it, or at least he didn't
mind doin' it once Red . . . I mean Dad . . . got him
started, and he hardly has ever gotten bigger, even
though we really do feed him, and I know he's not

deaf, like I told you, but he's never said a word, and I
guess he's really retarded. But I like the little guy."

And there are no accidents in heaven or in hell, and there are
no surprises. And I feel I am beginning to catch on, and there is
no way to be off the path except to follow too closely the bogus
maps sold by charlatans at the cathedral.

And we wind down the narrow hewn stairs in the dark, through
colder air and thicker, and there is no light enough to bother
opening your eyes for, and we wind down this mine shaft.

And there is a light, and it does come from beneath and around
a door. My first sight of it is sudden, below me as we come down
and around the circumference of this circular shaft, making
our helical path—a single strand, not terribly long, this must be
ribonucleic acid, maybe messenger RNA. And I am getting a
message, vibrations in my ears a bit too high-pitched for me
to hear (like a dog whistle, I suppose). I feel something like an
inaudible humming, and finally I feel "good vibes". They radiate
from behind the heavy door as if they will melt it.

20. Approaching The Boy

I don't remember terror because I never felt it. Others may be braver than I, or lucky to have suffered battle, madness, disaster, kidnapping, rape . . . or perhaps, come to think of it, they also often must obliterate memory, numb themselves somehow or another to avoid the truth of pain. So, they are not lucky at all, just hurt. It occurs to me (not without reason) we numb ourselves also to avoid the guilt and shame which come from having been victim. It doesn't make sense, but it makes sense to me that even when I have been hurt by someone else's callousness, cruelty, even sadism, I feel guilty as if I had done the bad act (as if I had set myself up, or even seduced the criminal into hurting me), I feel ashamed as if I were debased by someone else's abuse (instead of crying "Ouch!" or "Cop!" or "Stop!" I say, "Oh no! I am ruined."), and I seek to become numb, to avoid feeling, to avoid knowledge—all of which leads me to the grandiosity of denying I was hurt, as if I were invulnerable, "They never touched me. I never felt a thing."

I am approaching the boy I have been seeking, and I am having such thoughts! I am certain I am about to meet him, more convinced by how I feel than all I know—and I am imagining hidden hurts? It is as if my emotional armor were melting, those practiced habits of speech and gesture, mind and body which have made me successful in the world, those adaptations to conventional society which protect me from the slings and arrows. It is as if my emotional armor were melting like I imagine that heavy door before me is melting, the last barrier between me and my soul is melting, and I am ecstatic and afraid.

Even Rick is silent for a moment; and of course you, my Aegis, are eloquent in your wordlessness. We are at the door. Rick raps a rhythm on it with his knuckles. We wait. I hear my beloved cacophony (or assonance, if you wish) of Prokofiev's Third Piano Concerto, what had seemed to me real music before there was any such as rock and roll. We wait. The door simply opens and a veritable ocean of shimmering blue damask overwhelms my eyes, fills the cavern into which we step. Those silken curtains draped from the dome, above what is visible down to and flowing over the floor, whorl there like a bridal train upon the floral carpets whose hues are the forest's carpet of smoldering autumn leaves. Such dramatic fabrics on such an intimidating scale have suddenly made me feel I am in a large theater by surprise. I adjust my focus to center stage and on a large bed ornately carved with arabesques, in embroidered caftan and jewelled turban I see a little boy reclining amid sequined and intensely embroidered pillows, Serene Prince of the Entire Universe.

I am awed. Opulent furnishings have caught my eye, dragged it around the room a couple times, but what awes me is the dissonant relationship between the only person before me and the outrageous and incongruous environment he inhabits, his habiliments into the bargain. There is nothing here in the least offensive, just shocking because it is utterly other than whatever I have ever seen. Like Puss in Boots, he is the innocent, anomalously costumed and set into the role of the powerful and worldly. Because his innocence shows he is above guile, and his opulence shows he is above vulnerability, he seems godlike. He reclines perfectly still, as if he had never a need to move from where he is, as if it were not he who a moment earlier came to the door to open it (for there is no one else to have done it).

21. Time Together To Speak

Rick evaporates, and you outside the door leave me alone with the boy. I am pleased merely to stand at the vestibule of the chamber, merely to see that he is there, real before my eyes. I stare, dumb, for a long moment, look to have my eyes discern some fakery, visually to dismantle the appearance of naive majesty, to unmask the charade, bare it for what I know it is, to strip the boy of his princeliness, take him under my arm as my possession kicking ineffectuous, take him to my own place to tame him to my service, to become my child, my student, my disciple, my slave.

I laugh a little to myself to think of the idiotic assumption shared by those coarse pair, Rick and Red. They have so little imagination they imagine I would want the boy merely as a sexual object. Such impulses are not a part of me, I swear. I know I have sought him and that I need him, but his prostitution horrifies and disgusts me, to tell the truth, and although I am willing to pity him and to pay him, I have not the slightest desire to touch him. Besides, I cannot imagine me wanting a boy rather than a woman under any circumstances, and even though I do like women, generally, I would never traffic with a prostitute.

I smile and feel smug, so comfortable with myself this little moment I begin to have a sensation of tumescence, as if my penis were taking it into its head to mirror feelings beyond my acknowledged feelings—and awareness floods me suddenly! I am immensely sexually stimulated by the sight of the boy, who is a part of me. His quietness, his openness, his innocence stir me. I want to stir them. And I recall the fleeting thoughts I have reveled in a moment ago to strip him, to take him, to make him mine!—I have been wanting to rape myself!

In a faintness of clear-cut confusion I go limp, limp toward the bed, crumple crying. He comforts me, cooingly rocks me as if he could not see the aggression by which I have approached him. I know I should feel profoundly guilty, wish to, but I can only feel the firm warmth with which a small boy embraces a grown man. I cry in joy and helplessness, give myself over into his arms expecting to admit everything I have ever done wrong, to cry my guilt and shame long and hard, but also I feel I will be forgiven, and I really wish forgiveness. And he rocks me.

I do not know how long I have been floating here, but suddenly with certainty I remember my vague but vital mission:

> "I came to talk with you. We must have time together to speak at length. Can we do that now?"

> His head shakes a vigorous "No" as his hands wave a repeated and rapid "No way!"

> "But when and where? Tell me!"

> His index finger to his lips says, "Quiet, now."

> "But this is what my life depends on, and so, I think, does yours."

> He shrugs as if to say, "That's not all so clear to me."

> "Stop this pantomime!" I shout in frustration. "Just tell me what I need to know straight out, you sadistic little tyrant!"

> The tears which swell up in his eyes, like a swollen tide pulled out of the ocean by the moon, weigh down his little head just enough to make it droop a bit. Tears,

47

eyes, moon, head, tide and ocean say succinctly to me, "You have hurt me unfairly to have accused me of withholding from you anything, for have I not always given you more than you would accept? And haven't I always truly loved you, followed you to protect you, even when you have abandoned me?"

"Oh, my God! What a monster I am! In my selfishness I have demanded you speak to me when I know you have always been mute. You could not speak. I could not understand. I am so sorry! I am so sorry. I am so sorry . . ."

He strokes me and quiets me from my passion of abasement, but I sob and sob. He tries to quiet me, and as I carry on, his hands say, "Hush, now. Shush." And he becomes more anxious, the compression of my hand by his hands, his squeeze of my shoulder saying, "I really mean it. Quiet, now, or we will be in trouble."

Rick bursts through the door like a flashing cannon ball, a bowling ball rolling fast and whistling the still air through its finger holes, spinning, curving from hard english, at me as if I were the headpin in the tenth frame of a perfect game. He comes at me fast, hard, uncompromising and with a purpose. Also with a knife.

It is in me! Before I can think, it is in me, and out of me . . . and in me, and out of me, and in me, and out of me, and in me . . . I am frantic, cannot breathe . . . AND THIS IS PAIN! I don't want to understand anything any more—I just want to out of this pain! . . . away . . . away.

"Meet me at the mountain meadow. Wait for me there. I will come soon. Wait for me."

He has articulated these words exactly, calmly, sweetly, the boy who has never spoken a word. And although I hear him clearly, in my state I understand nothing, and can argue about nothing.

I am dead.

A QUIETNESS BETWEEN A MAN

AND HIMSELF

1. Serenity

Is death serenity? I thought it would be nothing or I thought it would be hell. I thought wrong, and I am not surprised, and I am not disappointed. I am very much alive and well—or, more exactly, I am very much dead and well, and feel alive. Rick stabbed me repeatedly in the chest and abdomen. My lungs both collapsed and I bled profusely into and out of my abdomen as if my aorta were transsected. I remember these events vividly, as if they were a moment ago, and although my feeling state is immensely different from then, it was a moment ago I was unspeakably pained and powerless, dying and dead. But now I am very well. I have no pain. I breathe easily, and move freely. And to hell with explanations.

It is a wood. It is familiar to me. I have a sense of where I am and who I am, although I will not take the energy today to explain these to you. It is a pleasure to walk leisurely through the rocks and trees, down the mountain a way to the high meadow. Although it is well into autumn, the sun is shining on me through the trees. The still air will not bite me.

I feel the certainty of the earth within my feet meeting the trail each lightly bouncing step. I taste the air move in and out of me, bearing in it the essence of all that is. I greet each tree serenely with a quiet nod, and each nods back to me acknowledgement of peace between us. Squirrels and chipmunks and rabbits and porcupines and deer pursue their businesses about me, performing as their natural lessons have taught them, unafraid of me now, accepting me in minimal glances, and as they are some or more smaller than I am, I feel about them as I would for playing children doing their businesses for themselves or with each other in a city playground. I feel, but rather than the abrupt electric fragmentation of each sensation I experienced when I was first erupting from my numbness, now I feel fully without any exertion. Rather than to put out sensory feelers to focus on each phenomenon as one might through a microscope, rather than to stare or strain to hear or sniff and analyze as if there were a gas chromatograph in my head, I sense passively, without effort, accepting what is about me, accepting me as belonging exactly where I am, opening the windows of me I had shuttered, to let the breeze of freedom come and go within me. I walk in silent joy this hello to the universe I live in.

The meadow is before me, no longer flat but roundly folded in about the stream meandering its middle. I am here and now I am here, but I am not mindless, remember how it was to have been here once before (or more than once?) and I can anticipate afternoon rain or the coldness of the night or the winter storm which will naturally come some time soon. Having nodded to each blade of grass, I gather branches from the wood surrounding me to make a shelter at the edge of the meadow, just within the outspread fingers of the kindly trees. Without anxiety I anticipate the coming of the boy. Until he comes I will be here.

2. Balsam Boughs

Balsam boughs beneath, thick branches above layer upon layer, like a green igloo my modest dome is home. The sun is still high, and I am developing an appetite. I don't question the harmony with nature which protects me and provides me what I need. I do not even fear my own wonder, for it will not destroy my awareness, merely entertain my mind. What looks right to me is right enough. To the stream where I imagine I can take trout easily enough, and I suppose I could, but perhaps I have no need of them. Wild onion bulbs, various greens (not really bitter), pine nuts, mushrooms, rose hips, no raspberries remnant from the spring but raspberry leaves and maple bark for tea, wild grapes, currants, gooseberries, snow berries, bilberries, buffalo berries, wild carrots, leeks, potatoes, wild asparagus, the rare bird's egg, grubs from under the first layer of mulch or under windfalls. I am amply provisioned by the generous world about me, but not any utensil or pot in which to cook. And thank you, Memory, for reminding me where we buried refuse when last here. (And I would be a little ashamed we did not pack it out, but it seems we left it for a reason. So what was unwanted and worthless has been buried like a treasure, to be sought and found and valued highly, after all.) A little looking, a little digging and I have three not very large but very useful cans to boil my water, to make my broth or tea, to boil an egg, to boil wild wheat and grass seeds into porridge. Some delicacies I shall wrap in wet leaves and cook among the coals. I am alive and well and growing and eating with my fingers with relish.

I can feel the cold, but it does not hurt or numb me. my shelter saves me from the worst of the wind, and the fire I keep keeps me from frozen fingers of wind freezing my fingers. Thick boughs are not a feather comforter but they are what I have, and what I have is enough for me. I sleep my first night as I did here that distant time a week ago or so. (Or has it been a year? I know no way to measure time beyond this day, its night.)

I know this man was unable to wait. I wonder why I smile at me. I don't need to wait now, or fret, be anxious, angry. I need only what is with me. I feel wealthy here, reclining in opulence. I awake and take myself along the stream, across the meadow, into the wood collecting food to feed myself, to store in case the coming snows will kill or cover what I need. I await the boy, scan the meadow for him as I make my way about. I know he will come because he said so, but even more deeply I know I must await him because it is what he told me to do, and I am glad to be doing what I have been told, since these instructions have come from someone I trust.

I trust! I trust? I trust. I have come to trust myself, my world, my fellows human and other than human. I have come to trust because I have worn out mistrust. I can no longer afford to stand in judgment of everyone and everything. When I had to tell everyone else what was right and wrong I could not trust any of them to follow my instructions, but now that I give no instructions no one disobeys me. I am not angry at anyone. I am not even angry at Rick for having killed me. He did what he did for his reasons, which I have no way of knowing (since he did not discuss the matter with me), and through no intention or action of my own I seem no worse for the trauma. I may be better off than ever I was. I feel better than ever I have felt, but I can't know if that is good. I can't at all know what is good. I have somehow been relieved of the knowledge of good and evil. Perhaps I have received the blessing of reversal of Eve's and Adam's curse. Perhaps much or all of human suffering comes not from labor (both manual and obstetric) but from the distress to mind, soul, body and society which comes from the conflict of having to be right. Polarity of values kills us, makes us kill each other. The truth is not within what is right or wrong, but in what is, which, like the weather, is forever changing.

It is snowing now, and I am to my hut to lie on my back and watch the arced branches cross each other against white sky, simulate forms of many animals, wave lightly in the wind, each fat fluffy flake of popcorn snow fall in its helical path unstraight, like a paired maple seed spinning groundward slowly. I scan the meadow for him, do not see him but feel him approaching calmly from somewhere, at some speed, to arrive at some time.

3. Snow

Snow falls softly sometimes, deeper than it sounds. It covers dreams, covers wishes. It even covers sins. Snow protects me, covers my shelter in environmentally kosher styrofoam. Out and about, my legs get wet, but when I come home the fire dries me after a time. I find enough firewood and food to get along. I am losing weight but I am not losing much of me. Solitude is not lonely, since I have a lifetime of events and persons to review if I wish, and it is smooth and easy to do so since my mind is clear and free to see without having to make judgments or emotional reactions.

> "An uneventful recovery! Recovery consists in nothing but events."—
> Oliver Sacks (my woodsy approximate quotation).

And you are correct, Ollie. Quiet, peaceful, smooth, but each moment an event of action to care for myself or carefully to consider the realities within which I live or joyfully to take it in my senses. It has been many days—I have no need to count, but probably about ten days—and I have seen no sign of the boy. I wonder if I will have enough patience to wait if he is much longer, and realize I do not need patience, merely a form of self-restraint to enable suffering. I am not suffering, and I am not restraining myself. I wonder if I can survive the winter, and realize I need not worry about surviving. This is not survival, but living. I am feeding and warming myself as a part of my living this day. The events are each brave bird who cheeps, each breathing-in I take, each cloud or overwhelming sky-engulfing bank of clouds which comes, each peeking-out of the sun, each slow night-to-night reshaping of the moon, each currant bush discovered in the snow with a few deep dried fruit, each song which comes to my heart and out of my mouth, each squirrel brave enough to listen to me sing without making its panicked screaming way to warn all other squirrels to run away also, each dark cloud of an elk herd crowding down from higher up the mountain appearing at forest's edge to feed at this meadow on their way farther down the mountain.

And I am not perfect, and my life here is not perfect. Sometimes I wish I had a dog.

And my life goes on in thankful satisfaction. And I await him until he will come, and I lay in a modest store to feed him. Bears bless me with distance. Their approach worries me some, for my food and for my safety, but they come no closer than to be within view, nor do I know how it is they come no closer. And I realize I am not living by my own power, nor do I understand how or why I am here, so I stop worrying because I don't know how things should be anyhow, and I couldn't make them right even if I knew. So I bless the occasional ursine wanderer with a silent salutation, "Good Bruno, good old bear-dog. Catch a rabbit. Dream good dreams. Bark at the moon, dog-bear, good old pal." And I am not alone here.

So go my days busy about my business, and so go my nights of tender resting in what is now a cave in the brush beneath thick snow beneath the trees at the edge of the snow-laden meadow. It has been some time—a month, perhaps?—and there has been no sign of anything or anyone except those of us who live here, no migrant elk, no migrant birds, no migrant boys. Although I know I need him as much as ever, and I consider what to do to make him come faster or whether I should consider something happened beyond his control to delay him (but how could he have any power or control?) or something which has hurt him or killed him—and in less than a moment again I know all is as it should be, and if not, it is not I who can change it, but what I can do is wait, as I was told and as I trusted. And I wait.

Sometimes deep winter's blasts keep me in my hut for days, and I cannot look for his arrival, and I cannot imagine how he might find me when I who made this hut often can hardly find it, its very top now below the level field of snow. At this time which otherwise would be the final deep killing desperation I wait and know I am okay even if my food is low and I have tried chewing branches and live mostly on tea, and I can wait because my sustenance is in truth, over which I have no power and of which I have no deep understanding. I just live in it.

4. Frozen

Deleriously serene, I leave this womb rarely because there is no food for me that I can find. Weak in my legs I cannot go far when I go. I know I will go to sleep in the snow and fade into a flat carcass, a dark smooth elevation in the white field, like a rock anchored in the earth, no longer fluid but frozen to be a rock anchored in the earth. I shall be a carcass . . . like that rock, there, that looks like a carcass . . . of a deer . . . here . . . is a deer frozen in the snow. She is the very self I saw in my imagination of my own real being dead. It is as if I lay here before me to sustain me. Although I believe I have achieved much stoic calm, in the face of food my body becomes so organizedly agitated it uses energy I cannot have, as if wildly spending on credit, drags the doe's sacred body to the hut—not so difficult, I guess, downhill over crusted snow.

Who is it who cares for this now living me, now living well? I know it is beyond a who, beyond a what, beyond a force, beyond the imaginable, beyond the unimaginable. I thank the ineffable, unnamable Thou who gives me life, who lets me cherish life even when I am ready again to accept my death. I weep in gratitude in my little den, I scream my realness into the vastness of all space, where you are not. And I do not feel insignificant to thank you, although you need no thanks, because it is best for me to give thanks, and to love you.

Now I have not only food for desperation, but meat I would not kill for myself. The deer must have fallen wandering abandoned from the herd, too high and cold to make her own way. Nor the bears nor the dogs nor the rodents have touched her. She must have fallen just last night, which might have been my last night. And now I have provision into spring, dressed and sectioned and buried deep in the snow beside my shelter.

And now from weakness I have strength, which transition I never knew because when I died before, I felt the pain but I didn't feel the healing. As soon as I have tasted the first raw meat (for I take my first meal off her thigh as soon as I have stripped away some skin, nor apologize to her nor you nor me) I have felt a thrill go from my mouth like warm spasms through my whole self, and even (I swear) in my dead numb frozen toes. And when I have first roasted some of her and dined at leisure I feel immensely satisfied. And realize I can make me hat and boots from her hide, and from my imagination and my hands' work, and from my confidence and care (for I will not have any skin to spare). This kind of demandedness is fun because it is real and necessary and exactly fitting with my life and needs today. If the unnamable provider provides the way, I must do the work which is my work. The reward is my being me. I have no need for indolence, which would be voluntary death, nor do I need to cherish secret anger that I have been demanded of, for no one is exploiting me. I thank you for the work which is before me.

Despite more snow whenever it must come, I feel it less cutting cold, not just because of my leggings but because there is a slow light mellowness in the air, and the nights seem shorter. By day I go about, find a few berries under the snow, strip bark and residual leaves for tea, renew the branches for my floor, dry wood for my fire, build step by step my tree-house tower better to scout his advent, and woven grasses and the hulls of nuts boiled into dye hang my flaming flag for him to see. Again I am full and self-sufficient through no power of my own and through the joy of my own small handiwork, the product of which is perhaps cute, but the process of which has saved me from dying by giving me a place in my own life.

5. Now Is The Time

Little snow, flurries at night sometimes. The top is crusty from diurnal sun. Beneath the crust a moist softness begins collapsing into drippings, dribbles, runnings, flushings, gurgles, flowings, springs, rivulets, small rivers under the disappearing snow, my styrofoam world melting as if touched with a burning match. I must leave my hut immediately, for it is flooded. I wonder at this intelligent sophistication within me which not only doesn't inform me, but hides the obvious away from me behind selfish grandiosity which assumed my unassailable home would be established forever as the center of the universe, my arrogant ignorance which assumed the melting snow would not dare make me wet. I laugh unendingly, gasp, collapse, gasp and laugh some more at this wonderful clown who brightens my day with his foolish antics. I move my possessions and provisions into the tower.

The tips of sticks are fat. Small animals scurry I have not seen in months. Snow is remnant only, deposited in brown banks. Wet earth is black and glistens. Fat sticks bud delicately the whitest shade of green. The ground does not freeze at night, doesn't crackle, squishes.

"You look good in a beard."

"I don't wear a beard, I just didn't shave this winter, and . . . It's about time you came. I've missed you."

"And I've missed you."

"And why am I not surprised for you suddenly to appear, so late, and grown up, I believe?"

"You are not surprised and I am not surprised because we have cared enough and survived enough to take away most of our expectations, our naïveté."

"You mean expectations are naïveté?"

"Is that what you mean?"

"You mean we mean the same?"

"Probably, now."

"Then why are we bothering to converse?"

"Is it a bother for you?"

"No. As I said, I have missed you. I feel I have spent all my life to now trying to make contact with you. I feel I need you, and I feel you need me. I mean, more exactly, I feel incomplete without having a sense of you, and I feel obligated to care for your vulnerability."

"Vulnerability? Man, we need to talk."

"Yes, thank you, that's what I mean, that we need to talk. I may not say things quite right the first try, but I know that what I mean to say is right."

"'Right'? Is that the best word for it?"

"Boy, you are demanding."

"And generous. Here, this pack is filled with food."

"Thanks, but I have plenty for both of us—and more is growing all around us."

"Then we are well provided for, and now is the time, and here is the place."

"Life begins anew each day. Thanks, Nameless."

6. I Am Not He

I smile amazed but not excited. I have no way to understand what happens, but now I have a way to accept whatever happens. It is he, but he seems entirely older, probably eighteen, and precisely rational. His surface hardly resembles the mute, timid, reserved, obedient little boy. I see it is he because the eyes speak from the same depth—different idiom but same depth. And no one else would come to me here and now. No one else would know to come.

We arrange our ample provender in the tree-house, use lines he brought to lift larger logs to extend the floor supported by two outreaching arms which are large branches of this massive fir, twelve feet above the runny soggy ground.

> "I had plenty of room for me up here, and thought there would be room enough for you also, even when I thought you were quite small."

> "We need more."

> "And I'm sorry I didn't thank you for all the food you brought, but I was so proud that I myself had gotten everything you might need . . ."

> "'Yourself'? 'Proud'?"

> "No, not 'myself' . . . nor 'proud'. I guess I meant I was glad to be able to give you what you might need, for your sake."

> "And you know what I need?"

> "Did you come to demean me?"

"And if I have?"

"I will learn to accept that also, for I accept you. I don't know why, but I don't know why not. It is my preconceived notion that I accept you as myself. It has not been easy to accept myself, much more arduous and repetitive than I had thought it would be, but accepting myself has let me live when I was dying (and perhaps when I was dead already), and accepting whatever is about me has allowed me a measure of peace. I have a need to accept you, but you are difficult for me to accept. You seem critical of me, and you are not as I expected. I sought and met a mute lad who had been hurt, used, abused, whom I could help, and although I know you must be he, you seem quite different."

"I am not he."

7. Questions Pendant

I fall into heavy puzzled silence, nor does he seem to need to talk nor resolve what seem to me heavy questions pendant. I have learned not to act angry, nor do I feel angry, but hurt somehow. I consider committing myself to silence until he speaks first, but I have no need for angry challenges. I am silent for a very long time because I do not have the slightest idea what to speak to him.

We cooperate very well without words, and I find these concrete construction tasks flow more than merely smoothly without words. It takes some internal freeing up of my willingness, but as I open I see and hear, and more than see and hear. We measure trees with our eyes, select them in our minds, fell them, move them, measure them and fit them with our heads side to side glancing, forth and back squinting, trim the trees, lift them into place, lash them tight, construct or tie in place walls or wind barriers of groundsheets or boughs. Thick lodgepole pines we wedge beneath each of our supporting branches to help them hold . . . Hold what? An army?

What I more than hear or see working with this youth in silence is how two bodies become one working together. I do not have to speak to ask him what he thinks we should do next. I come to know his movements before he moves, seek exactly the same tree or rock as he seeks it, know where it shall go and what we will have to do to have it there.

Even in the evening as together we cook our meal, we cook our meal in silence. I have a smoothly swimming sense of him with which I am in harmony. Finally covered away from the cold in sleeping bags in our dark shelter, my head sweetly spinning from the exertion of this day's work, all the finer senses narrowed to the dark and quiet body-stillness of reclining, I allow sound to come from me to him.

"Who are you?"

"You said you knew me."

"Now I do, having worked with you in silence, having eaten with you what you brought here, having experienced in me what my reactions are to you. Who are you?"

"You might call me a student."

"Are you angry at my foolishness?"

"You are no more foolish than I, I simply have been learning how to hide my foolishness behind learning."

"You are not the boy."

"No, although in a way I was he, as you were."

"And was I you?"

"Will I be you?"

"Perhaps because I have learned a bit to live, it will be a bit easier for you to live a bit."

"But you know I shall have to make my own way, my own errors, my own missteps on this path."

"It is a broad path. The places I have passed which seemed difficult have not seemed so when I have looked back. I don't know that life truly is a path, but if we talk of it that way, then it is the path of truth. I think of the little boy, how I would like to carry him along that path—and this wish is for me, selfish, to care for something in me, to carry myself along the path safe."

"You understand why I do not like that?"

"Sure, now I do. You resent generosity which is merely a guise for selfishness. You say, 'Do me no favors, especially if they are favors for yourself.'"

"Like a writer offering to read you his stuff."

"Do you think that's why the boy is silent?"

"He wants to be important to you. When all you want to do is give him things, do him favors, he fears he can do nothing for you, is afraid you want to buy him off, to silence him."

"Doesn't he know he is the most important, he is the most naïvely sensitive, that without him our sensations and sensitivities are coarse? Doesn't he know he is beautiful however he is, but most beautiful laughing and running? Doesn't he know for me to see him happy will convince me I was not bruised and silent when I was very young?"

"No. Of course he does not see things as you see them, nor as I do. I also will like to see him happy, but I am more likely to remind him life is cruel, to encourage him to keep up the silent act, deep tearless eyes, to suffer all that callous sadists offer so that they will not flare angry at passive defiance and kill him outright. I beg my baby brother stay alive. I love him!"

"How do you come to trust me enough to express your feelings wildly as a thicket growing thorny vines up and around each other tall as trees?"

"To protect the baby rose."

8. Free To Speak

Free to speak we remain silent mostly, communicating in our cooperation not with our faces only, more our bodies' attitudes. I do not know why we must build so much space in our camp, but I need not ask or question. Today I live in this day, so I enjoy the activity, sharing with him doing what we are doing. I consider the silence, how difficult it has been for me to accept it, to begin it—but I consider what silence had been for me, forbidden forbidding angry behavior not to be tolerated in society—and I thank God for my silence, the right to be without making noises. I remember a cat I inherited as a kitten (I had not volunteered to take care of him) who did not mew or cry or yowl even when stepped on unavoidably exactly under foot, lovingly walking across the house between my feet, (his naïve way of walking with me). This cat spoke only with his eyes and actions for all worldly purposes, but when he spoke to me or you personally it was in an immediate, spontaneous and voluminous purring which poured like honey at his being touched or petted or brushed or fed or held. I often held him to the phone to speak his loving rumbling purr across the country where it might be needed that day. Oh, that I might communicate all practical matters through my face and body and action, and that the only sound I need to make, the only words I need compose, be loving low quiet purring which you could hear happily comfortably interminably!

By now the tree-house tower can easily hold three to sleep, and at least three more on the platform under the tree—anchored, solid, level and dry, abutting the stone-lined fire-pit, grill, spit and wood pile where we can cook and warm ourselves. Perhaps this is a place where we could stay many and a long time. I have survived alone here what I thought would kill me. And now with momentous momentary panic I fear what will happen if this mountain meadow home should become inhabited by humans, civilized, what a cesspool it would become. In my mind civilizing humans are savages, tend to ravage the living loving world which is delicate as a kitten, a child, a rose.

9. Silver Space-Ships

"Shall we build more and more? I enjoy working with you, being with you, but I have no idea what is our task. If we do this for the pleasure of doing this, I say 'Good!' for I enjoy the doing of it, and might become good at it with enough practice, and feel good about myself that I am so able. Or are we trying to accomodate an immense party who will come in silver space-ships to join us here, soon to dismount the mountain, infiltrate the cities on the flatlands truly to civilize humankind with Venusian wisdom?"

"More the latter than the former."

"Thanks for the answer, but it is too sparse for my magnanimity (literally, my large mind)."

"Specifically, three others of us are coming."

"And who are they?"

"Who are we, you mean?"

"'We' includes me?"

"'We' always includes 'I'."

"' . . . more the latter'? Jokingly I asked if Venusians will come in silver space ships to infiltrate humankind to truly civilize them, and you say 'we' includes me. Am I a Venusian infiltrator without knowing it? And if so, how wise or civilizing can I be without awareness or knowledge? Look, I feel I failed in many ways as a 'civilized' human earthling, and I don't know if I want to risk being a Venusian on earth right now. I'm just not up to it."

"I do love you, you fool! But you have a few things inside-out, as usual. Yes, you are a part of us, and yes, our purpose is a sort of salvaging of humanness, but we are not from Venus (although love may benefit from our efforts). There are no secrets, no mysteries. You know all these things, but, it is true, your awareness has been damaged many times along the path."

Fully it is spring. Animals I had not seen in a long time have become visible to me again. A subtle splash at the stream turns my head—in the water all the blacker because the banks are still white with stubborn patches of snow, a sleek water rat is swimming.

10. I Wonder

I wonder. There are so many questions, I cannot formulate discretely even one. I am resting in the dark, not sleeping, not restless, but focusing on the little I know, the littler I understand. I am included—that feels good. The purpose is to salvage humanness—that sounds good. But who are these persons, and how do I come to be associated with them? And what, specifically, is the task here, what values to be promoted? And what has any of this to do with me, surviving here waiting for the boy? And why here? Why will any group of any sort choose to be here for any purpose? And what sort of coincidence brings them to where I am?

And now my wonders wander to a darker, colder clime. I wonder what can be wrong here. I wonder what secret cabals are conspired in. I wonder in what way I will be exploited, how I might defend myself or evade them. I fear for me.

And now I form convictions: that they have found me here by no accident, that they have been looking for me since I left my job, left that distant city "burnt out" and vulnerable, that they intend to use me to procure drugs under my unused license, to get all they can before they are detected, that when no longer useful to them I (who disappeared abruptly from there previously on my own) will disappear again, in pieces down the sewer! Having decided these sorts of things, it is easy for me further to ascertain they are the DEA.

I am, of course, now restless and distressed. Thank God I have been learning not to believe these sorts of certainties. It only takes a moment for me to know these are untrue. But I still feel bad about them. I feel bad about what is not so, what only happened to me in my mind! So, what is new? We tend to act this way above the nose, between the ears. Not to worry. "Just say 'No'."

I reconsider. He came to see me. He knows the boy. He seems to be his brother. He says others are coming. Will the boy come? He told me he would meet me. It is spring. My life is good exactly in proportion to my trust. I have been blessed by untrusting thoughts tonight, paranoia, to which I am no longer a victim, a human sacrifice. I have been reminded that the only thing I have learned, the only thing I know to do, is to trust despite the seeming imperfections of the universe—for I cannot judge them, and I cannot repair them, but perhaps I know who can, and that's the one I trust, and I sleep like a rosy baby, like a sleek curled kitten.

11. Empathy

"What do you study?"

"Philosophy mostly."

"Which philosophers, especially?"

"Kierkegaard, Plato, Buber, Aristotle, Leibniz, Kant, Hegel, Hobbes, Nietzsche, Ashleigh Brilliant . . . I've read lots of them."

"Are you in a university?"

"I have been, but I find it too difficult to study there. Institutions corrupt even the most honest professors. The ones I know could have helped me when they were students no longer have what I seek. They have fallen prey to departmental politics and administrative demands, are too busy putting together papers to be printed to put together ideas. They have come to demand the right answers from students rather than the right questions from themselves."

"And what is it you seek, which can no longer be found in universities?"

"The truth."

"The truth?"

"Look, I'm not so naïve as you treat me. You have asked terse questions of me about myself. You should know, if the questions are honest, there are many levels of truth in the answers, that any response I give can unfairly be attacked. Questions and answers are not to be attacked, but to be, to be studied, to be rearranged indefinitely (if need be) to show something new, or more importantly something new about something basic. I don't know if you can understand the simple things I am saying, but if not there is no need to discuss any of it, so let's not."

"You have stated well in your words and in your emotional expression that you feel abandoned and misunderstood by the men you wished to look up to, that you fear it will be the same with me."

"You have cut me to the heart! Thank you."

"You are certainly welcome. It is a privilege to be able to understand you, or, more exactly, to empathize. 'Sympathy' is 'feeling (or suffering) with' but 'empathy' is 'feeling in'. In other words, all the American professionals have it backwards (not surprising) to consider empathy to infer the maintenance of ego boundaries intact, therefore 'good'. And I say it is my privilege to have my own attention to your words and action result in my apprehending your "existential" state as if I myself felt it, 'feeling in' you, empathizing— and to hell with 'ego boundaries'. So, you like to read philosophy alone?"

"And I'm beginning to like you, too."

"Reading philosophy, or doing anything else important, alone is difficult, dangerous."

"You mean because one might not understand enough without a teacher?"

"No, you might understand too much, might read into it more than is there to be understood. That might be too much like thoughts in solitary confinement with no book at all, or a winter's delirium isolated on a mountain top."

"Then you are saying isolation subjects us to many thoughts, but they may be madness. And you imply that reading in isolation is very close to that, the text but a frail tether to reality."

"Yes, and a beloved tether which willingly I wear about my neck as if it were of gold and diamonds and kept my head from falling off, for I swear some of my dearest friends (not all) are those you have named, and if it were not for the respect with which I cherish their actual words I might appropriate or pervert them. These persons are real and intimate to me—like Aristotle who has come down the hallway toward me at three in the morning crying, 'Kenneth, poor Kenneth . . .' and I have said, 'But, beloved Ari, you are the one who has been most profoundly misunderstood. Why pity me, who have written little to be misread?' and he, 'But you will suffer more, and I am already dead.'"

"You really do know Aristotle, don't you? You know his soul."

"It lives."

"And if there is danger in isolated thought, and peril in isolated study, does that mean I must return to the university?"

"Not 'must', nor avoid solitude or solitary study, but be cautious about harm you may do yourself. Harm from others you can hardly control without becoming narrow, selfish and paranoid (and when you have become thus insane, you have yourself done it). It is to ask, 'Is this what I need to do, how I need to be?' and if you find it is not for you, to do something else—and I do not mean change professions, but in each momentary act be yourself. That's all you get. That's all there is for you."

"I appreciate what you seem to be trying to tell me . . . I mean, I really do like a part of what I hear . . . I mean, you . . . oh, I mean . . ."

"You mean what I know already—I preach when I say more than three words a day. I don't like it either, but I haven't achieved the level of serenity to slow it down. I apologize."

"You certainly know Aristotle intimately. You are the very peripatetic."

"You have touched my heart. Thank you."

"It makes sense that the finest work will come about in community, but I doubt that often happens. Institutions of all sorts are dysfunctional, foster competition rather than cooperation. I can't work that way. I have never found even one person with whom it was really easy to work. I haven't even found anyone with whom to live. I thought I was okay being independent and competent, but your suggestions bring me to question that."

"You realize I have no answers, that my familiarity with the questions is all I have so far. You see I am not living in community. I, too, left society because I was perishing there even when I was 'successful'. I have come to believe in 'community' but I don't know that it will ever exist for me."

"Today two isolated from society, seeking community which may not exist . . . and here we are, working together, communicating without words, communicating the most complex words, surviving! You know, we just may have got us a piece of it."

12. Twin Specks

Silver space ships descend through spring sky's morning brilliance, bringing down to earth something of loving, to do some humanizing by means of Venusian wisdom . . . or something like that.

My early morning scanning of the meadow gives me two new radar blips, specific specks far up at the edge of the meadow, edging down slowly together. Fully the time it takes to make my tea and crackers it takes the twin specks to make their way close enough for me to see they are not only two but larger and smaller. The youth and I look together from the tower. I ask if he knows who they are. Perhaps he does. I ask if we should go to meet them. He sips his tea.

I am absolutely befuddled because, as the student has told me, I know everything but I can't remember or understand, so even though I have a sense that everything is coming about just the way that will be best for me, for everyone, my anxiety is excitement to be here in the next moment and the next, to experience each event, each moment, each thought, each sensation, each meeting, each doing. This is the excitement of being alive today in the here and now. I am happy, even though I know I know nothing of what will be. I trust the future, feel unjustifiedly securely who I am, how I am. I remember Kierkegaard's essay "The Unhappiest Man" in which he showed the unhappiest man anticipated the past and remembered the future. The implications came to me after a time of study and consideration. One who anticipates the past is preoccupied with ancient history, studies it as if it holds all value, seeks to understand it as if it were ever-changing and required constant scrutiny. To remember the future is to know already what cannot be known, a form of "knowledge" which can only be madness, utterly severed from reality. So the unhappiest man looks for change or growth in what is fixed and unchanging, and he looks to the unknown with a yawn (for he lives the existential stance he already knows all), and the unhappiest man cannot be in the present, he cannot be alive. But I am alive this moment, and I do not have to know or to remember in order to do it—I live it!

"Hello! Come here! Can't you see my red flag? Hello! Welcome"

"They see us, so stop your histrionic gesticulations, if you will."

"You are the stodgiest adolescent in three counties! There are no neighbors to be disturbed nor anyone before whom to be embarrassed, so get real for once—Please forgive me. I am sorry to have barked at you, even in excitement and with humor of a heavy sort. They are coming closer, slowly. No wonder slowly, his legs are so short and the meadow soggy under foot and deep in last year's grass. His legs are so short, and . . . of course, it is the boy! Beloved child, my heart melts and my eyes flow. Exactly whom I expected, and to recognize him suddenly thrills me with immense surprise and joy. And see here (my brain is working, albeit slowly as mud) some large person gently and patiently guiding him, not dragging him apace (as I have done to others often in my mania, haste and choking panic), not even carrying him like a baby (as I have wished to do), but walking with him as a companion, her whole body showing she focuses on the boy who is with her rather than on this still distant flag or us here in the tower whom she can see now. The large person is truly companion to the small. That large person is my companion! She is my beloved Virgil, Buddha, Sancho Panza, silent guru, zoo keeper, punching bag, confidant, Tonto, Aristotle, devilish tormentor, truest friend! These are my beloveds coming true together. This is my happiest day!"

13. Real Coffee

I am pleased at my excitement, as I am pleased at my serenity. By the time you have both made your way into the camp, and we four are together in the same place for the first time, I am quite calm. My pleasure is quite full and real and here and now without gushing. I embrace you each, and you each other silently (of course), and even my haughty stodgy student hugs me and hugs you and skitters up to the tower with the boy—and don't boys love tree-houses!—and they chatter (all with one older voice, almost fully baritone) and I can see with my heart's eye the little one peering over the railing to see how far out the world goes (but much more intensely peering down to see how far down the spit goes), scuttling with his feet excited to imagine it is a fortress from which he can defend himself against savage white men or infidel crusaders, neutralize enemies with his blow gun and his ray gun. We are home.

Dear friend, we sit and sip real coffee you have brought. Your presence strengthens me. And I am silent. I have no need for words. At first I have considered I should tell you what has happened since I saw you last where I was killed and the continuity of my awareness was disrupted, but then I know you know already, or if you wish to hear you'll ask. And silently we sit in sunshine watching the birds and rabbits, being with each other. The stream gurgles, occasionally emits the swishing of the swimming water rat or the splash of a jumping frog. ("A confused megalomaniacal toad?" I wonder whimsically.) New green shoots of grass delicately punctuate the crushed brown mat of last year's spears, now flat. Discontinuously beneath it there are rustlings, risings, fallings under the bracken—mice, I imagine for the fast ones, and for the slow ones moles. Behind us in the woods I spot a handsome gruff badger businesslike traversing territory which had been hers, grumbling at our intrusion, but too wise to take the matter into her own claws.

A RAUCOUS CONVERSATION AMONG
A MAN AND HIMSELVES

1. We Are Five

"How long shall we be waiting for her? That is my rhetorical question, since we know we never know."

"I don't know how I do it over and over again, waiting for her, tolerating her outbursts, her impulsive behaviors, bailing her out of one jam into another. She thinks her father was so conservative and reserved. If she only knew! He was my friend, it's true, but so many times I had to rescue him from the most outrageous scrapes. I have said over and over I will not live that way again—and as I have become much older than anyone I know, than anyone at all for all I know, I have been hooked into the scams and schemes rarely—but here I am again waiting for her, and You-know-who knows why."

"Well enough for you two to have your judgmental attitudes, but for all your knowledge and your wisdom you don't know why as well as I. It is this simple: She is exciting. I don't know how to analyze as you do, don't know all the pieces of the reasons. I only know it is thrilling to be with her, unpredictable, sometimes

frightening but always electric. When I am
with her I know I am alive."

And so those three friends, my visitors, speak of
someone I do not recognize—perhaps the fifth of us
the student meant as we worked day to day to make
our camp out of what had been my hut. Or perhaps
he meant something different when he said, "We are
five." Perhaps he was making an oblique play on
words, that we would somehow fall just one short
of Now We Are Six, like the well-formulated (but
not very funny) joke about the man who invented
Six Up. All I know is I don't know . . . No, that's
not all. I also know it's all okay with me. Don't
mind me, I just live here.

Getting to know them better just by being with
them, I am coming to love them each uniquely,
substantially and surprisingly ever-changingly. I
never really knew anything about my companion on
my previous journeys except that I needed her to
complain to, relied on her to accept me, accept
my anger and confusion, sensed somehow her age
must contain much kindliness and wisdom. About the
little boy I knew absolutely nothing, had never
seen him, just believed for no rational reason he
was alive somewhere, and if I followed my feelings
I would find him. The youth surprised me, but I
found myself empathizing with him and admiring
him. I would never wish to change him as he grows
along his own path. I love him for who he is, and
maybe for who he will be in the world.

I don't know how winter went away. It was completely
out of my control throughout. I began my stay here
thinking I could provide for myself, thinking my
stay would be brief, limited. I almost died again
(perhaps I really did die) and learned some more

of how to make my living. I learned there are no limits to living, that it is always worth doing despite any terrifying conditions, that living is better than sex. I learned there are no limits to living, that although uncertainty and pain are always present, when I accept them as unlimited conditions for me I am more free than I would have been, that pain and privation are no more devastating than the weather—and I adapt myself to the weather, because I cannot begin to change it, nor would I care to try to do so ever again.

I don't know how winter went away, nor how it can be spring now. Any word I say of spring will have been said a trillion times by any one any where any springtime. I won't speak spring, but live it.

And isn't it puzzling . . . ? Somehow step by step and suddenly, as winter evaporated and spring grew into the mountain I began to learn names in my heart of those closest to me, those three talking over there: Dear Badger, Wonderful Water-rat, and Baby Moley.

2. The Wind In The Willows

As I recall, Kenneth Grahame was born in privation, was born in Scotland, was raised by a strict grandmother, wished to study classics and literature at Oxford but having an entrée into the ground level of the Bank of England through an uncle was compelled by his internal family and external family to take the bank job. He became the youngest Director ever, which gave him some status and freedom for a while, including the freedom to write essays which tended to reminisce toward childhood. His only child, the sickly child of a sickly marriage, born late in his parents' lives, was run over by a train early in the second year of his second school away from home—what today would be recognized as a teenage suicide. Kenneth had made up stories for his son about the various animals of rural England he had learned in his own childhood and his continuing love of the outdoors, walking. He had written little or nothing of the animal stories during his child's lifetime, but began the writing after his pneumonias took him out of the Bank. Perhaps he found the task of writing <u>The Wind in the Willows</u> a painful one, both for his child and for the child within. It is considered and treated as a classic, often considered a children's book, but recognized by those (probably many, probably secret) adults who have read it as various things, but hefty (as was Mister Grahame).

<u>The Wind in the Willows'</u> story is of Mole, Ratty and Badger who try to protect, tame, keep up with, love and understand the impulsive (probably manic) Mister Toad. It is worth reading, or if you are isolated on a mountaintop for the winter, for you it is worth writing. Toad has or does the exact equivalents of getting and getting carried away with a customized van, a speed boat, several of the latest model sports cars and a Lear Jet. In his manic (and certainly drunken) escapades he steals a car and is imprisoned. While he is up the river evil weasels and stoats commandeer Toad Hall and trash it in their prolonged debaucheries. Toad escapes from prison (naturally) and the four friends arm, sneak into Toad Hall through the secret back tunnel and pummel the dangerous armed drunken villains, reclaim Toad's ancestral home, and subdue the stoats into unwilling servants. The story does not end in any stability, for it is clear Toad is still Toad, and no one can know what will happen next. Or something like that.

A few of the aspects of <u>The Wind in the Willows</u> which occur to me today to be notable or unique are: (a) Its use of animals with human characteristics (predated by Aristophanes and innumerable others) allows them more fullness, including imperfections or character deficits, more individuality and more interpersonal interaction of an emotionally delicate and realistic sort than any previous such animal story. (b) Its animal characters are not just humans in animal masks, but despite fidelity to human character, emotion, fault and pathology these animals also retain at least residual loyalty to their own species' characteristics. (c) Despite the risk of fixed stereotypes in relationships and characters, and the risk of coarse wish-fulfillment in adventures and heroics, Grahame is sufficiently humanly imperfect to fail to polish these into perfect literature, leaves things hanging or painful enough to leave me believing this story feels something like real life.

The impact of <u>The Wind in the Willows</u> on my life and thinking this morning can be summarized in a single idea: Animal characters humanized can be a medium to reflect that animals strive to survive through evolution and genetic programming (Aristotle's "by nature"), whereas humans tend to subscribe to produce and value artifacts and societal rules, believe convention will save them from the exigencies they avoid (Aristotle's "other causes" and my "unnatural"). Long ago I learned to isolate myself from society, mistrusting its seeming killing of my self. Recently I have learned I am an animal, and must realize it in action, actualize my animality, or die. Individual animals seem to cooperate in survival of species, whereas humans seem willing to do anything to survive as individuals. Natural endowment, not consciousness of self, seems to motivate animals, not humans. But these rigid dichotomies are false. Each of us who lives lives as a self, and lives in every sort of relation (especially spiritual) to every other living being. By nature we are each of the species of the living.

3. Waiting

Today we four lie in the sunshine unafraid. We wait for her, but we are unanxious. We know we haven't the slightest shadow of a chance to make her come sooner or to stay or to be serious even for a moment or to "behave" in any way. I remember when I waited for my grandmother, wondered if she would have Juicy Fruit gum for me. I remember when I waited for my professor, wondered if he would grade my composition high or low, if he would come to the coffee shop with me to talk about it. I remember waiting for the boy, the huge emotions having violently and heroically sought him over, empty of energy, patient, accepting, trusting he would come his own way. And I realize I am finding within myself the sorts of feelings each of my friends is experiencing now in waiting for Toady. Young Mole is excited, can hardly contain himself anticipating new pleasures he cannot himself imagine, must depend on Toady to bring to him. Ratty wants acknowledgement and sharing, but must maintain his reserved aloof arrogance. Badger is very like my grandmother, gruffly tut-tut-tutting at indecorous behavior, but never imposing discipline, always absolutely loving, but never confused about the values which have been delicately fixed by a full lifetime of awareness, experience and doing–and patient, patient.

Waiting together is easier than waiting alone. And every time I check, life is more wondrous and love is more abundant.

"Remember when Toady taught us all to dance?"

"Oh! What a time! I was so young I can hardly remember clearly. I remember spinning and spinning and bouncing. I was dizzy–drunken dizzy. I never knew I could move so, being used to crawling slowly through the earth, under turf, at home in the loam, a bore, not a child of Terpsichore"

"Oh, Moley, how prolix you have become."

"What is 'prolix'?"

"In your case, just wonderful. I've never heard you speak so. You certainly are excited that Toady is coming. I am too. Thanks for showing me so much how I feel. I'm beginning to admire your emotional honesty. I love you."

"Oh, what a time it was, dancing with Toady. She even tried to drag this old hulk onto the floor, and almost did. And no one sat and tapped her feet as fast as I did then. She is an inspiration, after all–no one more misbehaved, no one more loved."

"Now, Badger, you know not everyone loves our Toad. Remember when she was in school she infuriated the teachers, never did what was assigned, disrupted the class with her antics . . . But I honestly believe it wasn't because of the authorities' disapproval that she left school. I don't think she has ever been aware in the least of the disapproval she gets from others. I think she left school simply to be dancing on down the road. She never looks back."

"Oh! Do you think she'll leave us like that, never look back?"

"Moley, wipe your eyes and blow your nose. Toady loves us best of all, and you especially. No matter where she goes or for how long, Toady will always come back to you, as long as she lives and maybe longer."

"I love her more than anything . . . but I love you too, Ratty, and you, Badger dear . . . and Kenneth, I love you."

"And I love you, you beautiful Mole."

4. The Wind

Truth in any of her seemingly capricious forms challenges my claims I have made peace with her. I claimed life is always beautiful, and I was right, but I have to prove it repeatedly. Even my winter seemed wonderful in retrospect when spring had come, and certainly this lazy day in the sunshine together has been beautiful, like a vacation from real time. But now is now, and is her own truth, defiant of convention or expectation.

I didn't know such events could occur in the weather. Even in an antarctic winter there is some limitation of the forces and temperatures, but as soon as I saw the straight black line across the sky, and saw that line was moving straight as a blade, I knew all hell was about to break loose, and here it is!

The temperature is dropping fast, like a brick on my foot. The wind already is such a punch against me I must brace myself to stand, and that not for a moment more. We are all lying on the deck . . . No! Ratty is not here. Could he be . . . ?

> "Ratty! Come down out of the tower! Now! Can't you hear me?"

The wind is too sudden and too outrageous. Everything we have is gone! I can't see a shred of a sleeping bag, a tarp, a branch of our walls, pots, pans, my brilliant red flag—all blown away, scattered in the trees and rocks. The deck and the tower are in one moment cluttered, the next moment clean, the next moment half gone. Only the trees stand, and not all of them, and prone (not standing) three figures lie, grasping the deck with their hands and feet and faces (and I am one), and one grasps hanging from the remnant of the tower. Oh! beloved Rat, poor precarious rag flapping! My God! What will happen now?

Now Rat crashes, a limp and broken heap.

"Ratty! Ratty, speak to me."

"rrgffrr"

"What did you say?"

"I said, 'Rare gopher.'"

"'Rare gopher'? What does that mean?"

"adunno, buddid wuz alli cudsay a momennago."

"Are you alive?"

"I thingso."

"Poor boy! You're leg is broken, almost bent in half in the middle."

"Yes, and OUCH!"

"That was some far drop."

"Morally, at least. I was higher than any of
you a few minutes ago. This is a physically
humbling experience."

We must save ourselves, but we are powerless.
The killer wind has quickly abated to a gale, but
the rains are upon us cold. The dark is cavern-
black, but lightning scares us flaring, and is so
bright erupting incandescent from the murk it is
like flashbulbs in your face or reading 'Sylvania
120 Watts' while the lamp is on. The thunder is
oppressive, like living in a drum, but is not so
frightening as the crackles, the little parts of
lightning I have never heard because I have never
been so close. It is the sound of electrically
frying eyes or toes or other small delicate people
parts.

Togetherness is not just in living together, but
perhaps more in staying alive together when you
actually need every tooth and toenail to hang on
to the surface of the earth and each precious
other. We gather about broken Rat because he
cannot move to gather about us, and we must gather
together. Mole cries, reminds me of the boy who
would not. Perhaps we are all crying, but no one
can tell since our faces are all flowing in the
homogeneous dense shower.

"I hope Toady has not come. She is so
delicate and feminine, I am afraid she'd
perish."

"I am afraid we'll perish."

"No way. We've come this far and we've come
together. We'll go together. Whatever may
be the forces which assail us now, they

have no animosity for us. Nor are they friendly. This is the world we live in, and it will not kill us, nor will it save us. We must be ourselves here, do what we must to go along with these conditions until they are easier for us to withstand or avoid. We are together and alive, and we will meet with Toady. We must, because it is who we are to do it, in this life or another."

5. The Wake

The wake of the storm is disaster indeed. Every little thing we had is gone, and all that is left us is chill and mud and splinters. The rain continues steadily, the wind whirling it about in its frantic dance, the floor-length skirt and petticoats arcing ever-changing continuous patterns. The dark sky precipitously deepens its darkness through bleak evening, any next moment to become utter lightlessness. Now indeed we have nothing but each other. This morning was bright and warm, we had all we needed, more than we wanted, and now we haven't even the slightest food to share nor a way to prepare, we haven't even a dry or warm place to sleep, nor can we retreat from the mountain in a march like the precipitous one I made from here a few months ago, for one of us is too severely broken to move from this now desolate place. So we huddle together in the wet and dark and cold. And we are satisfied with what we have because it is exactly what is here for us now, and we do not compare it with other places or other times past or future. This is what is for us, and we are glad to be together. We have splinted Ratty's leg and bound his wrenched shoulder in a sling. We hold each other close together, and even though we can hardly sleep now, we spend no energy on talking. We need silence now, just to save energy for first light, long hours away, when we may know what will be open to us.

Unfortunately, the night does not surprise us. It continues cold rain and black earth eclipsed by clouds from her beloved celestial bodies, as in time of war a young woman sadly may be separated from her soldier-lover, and no one knows if they will ever again shine light each into the other's face. And we are welded together by love and necessity, and isolated into a harsh now. And the sleeplessness and the silence let me try to remember and wonder at what has happened to me and about me and in me. And I cannot know or understand, but by now I am getting used to being in the dark, so I wait until a light comes to me to illuminate my way. Perhaps some day I shall know something of who I am, but for now I shall wait, and be thankful I am alive.

6. Precipitously To Descend

Bright sun comes as if she never knew how dark this world is supposed to be . . . but maybe she knows something I do not. So, why argue with her? Who am I to argue with the sun?

"Ratty, are you still alive?"

"I am alive, certainly, for hell cannot hurt this much. Yes, this is it, the same old world again."

"Ratty, Ratty, are you well again today?"

"No, Moley, not well, but happy to see you well. Your little face is radiant with the sunshine, sharp needle teeth gleaming, wet black fur pawed in centrifugality from your eyes and mouth, and that center is your delicate pale nose. Lean it closer. Let me kiss you lightly right on the tip of it."

"I have an idea (although I am skeptical of my own ideas). It is warming. It will be a bright way down the mountain, slowly, and we can make it."

"What! We can't leave Ratty here!"

"But we can carry him. We can make a litter. Badger and I can carry him, head and foot. Moley can go ahead to be our scout. It will be slow, but nothing holds us here."

"One thing does, Kenneth. We have been here to wait for Toad."

"We can leave a message, here at the wreck of our camp, that we have gone down the mountain. She will not miss it, and she will know we are still alive, and there is only one road down. We might even meet her coming up."

"What became of the serenity which sustained you waiting here through the winter? You told me you had found spiritual capacities in yourself you had never before experienced, and now I fear you are ready precipitously to descend this mountain, as you did when you dragged me last summer to the flatlands, to the city, to your death."

"Thank you, beloved friend. I have forgotten neither the events nor the experiences. I had reminded me to go slow, and as I told you, this is just an idea, of which I also am skeptical. But what shall we do? I don't know how to believe poor Ratty can be repaired here—we need a surgeon for him. I do not know how we can survive staying here without equipment or provisions. I am afraid for Little Moley as I never was for me through the winter. I am afraid for Ratty. For you and me, dear old Badger, I only hope when the earth swallows us some time soon she will be nourished well. I

hope I have lived well or honestly enough,
at least recently, the earth will not spit
me out like a bad pistachio."

We take each other seriously and consider. We have no argument among us, but weigh back and forth what seem the varied valences of our possible courses. Sun shines and consideration proliferates. All in a moment we see Mole hold his little belly in his paws. His simple monosyllabic squeak is the clincher. Discussion abruptly stops. Badger and I are out into the meadow to find roots and young grasses, Mole into the trees about the camp to salvage bits of what we had lost. First things first, we must have food. Mole's direct expression of natural feeling has reminded the cerebral verbal aspects of us how we really feel, this moment in which we live. We will meet fears of the future later, or never, if we hold on to the faith humility offers us.

7. We Wait

We wait, or more exactly, we live this moment welcoming the next. When our own tiny fears, huge in our own minds, are set aside, we are freer to be. Repeatedly we do the setting aside, daily perhaps, or even each moment, and with fear out of the way for a while we live in blind confidence—the best and truest kind. Ours is anything but self-confidence, for even though it is ourselves who have confidence, our confidence is in something quite other than ourselves, something we cannot know or control or conjure up. So, ironic, contradictory and transcendental as it may seem, we wait unafraid, and while we wait we are free to begin doing what we need to do to care for our selves. We find food, rebuild shelter, reassure each other by our presence, and wait for Toady as we said we would.

The day passes peacefully even though each of us is busy. Moley is not a bad scavenger, finds this and that among the rubble of the immeasurably furious storm. What he finds, even bits and pieces, he brings to immobile Ratty to piece together or to clean of mud. Badger and I are busy searching and digging for whatever may nourish us, for wood to dry in the sun so we may soon again have the comfort of a fire to warm us and to boil up a vegetable stew in the pot Mole has retrieved with his heart-warming holler. And we do gather warmly and tired about our fire pit, we four drink warm broth from two mugs and a tin can, and again the meadow has been a kind home.

Morning again bright and warm after a night of deep sleep, everything seems peaceful except Ratty's angry leg shouting at him even when he lies still and shouting at all of us when he moves the least bit, red and redder at the swollen crater where ragged bone stabbed through. Everything seems peaceful and easy compared to how it was during the storm, compared to how it might have become had I dragged us down the mountain. Everything seems peaceful until . . . I hear a shouting as if somewhere in the back of my head, just to the right of center, small and distant as if I had a closet in the back of my head and an angry fly were stuck there under a blanket, behind a box of photographs, reverberating a tennis racquet, the thick door closed tight and locked. And now the shout I thought imaginary and inaudible is barely audible and nagging, but I can make nothing of it. And now the persistent little shout takes on a pattern less than random, phrases itself in muffled Turkish. And now the shout has pattern like an emerging bud unfolding its petals, still too pale to state its color or its shape, a gooing baby. And now Badger, and now Ratty seem attentive to my private auditory hallucination, cocking their heads rigidly one degree to left of center, saying nothing, listening, withholding judgement as to the meaning or the message—too distant, too faint. And now Moley shouts,

> "Toady! Toady is coming! I hear her! Where is she?" and distant shouts become clearly audible,

"Moley! Little Moley, where are you? Ratty! Sleek quick Ratty, show your face. Badger! You big old grump, come give me a hug before you criticize me. Kenneth! Kenneth, I have been looking for you. No more hide and seek. Come out, come out wherever you are!"

And It Is Toad!

We peer every direction, since sounds echo every which way off the mountain and the rocks and the thick wood. We peer communally, eight eyes scanning eight directions, and simultaneously we focus on an amazing object, a bright yellow gypsy wagon pulled by a horse, driven by a figure sitting high in the driver's box dressed in a bright yellow frock, wearing a bright yellow bonnet, holding a bright yellow parasol in one hand and in the other the reins—the most flamboyant and glamorous platinum blond toadette I have ever seen.

8. Goodies

Monica Toad is special. She is so delicate and feminine she must have help off the driver's box, which the three of us clamber to offer, and Ratty straining to sit since he cannot stand.

"Goodies for everyone!"

As she brings out a plate of cookies still warm from baking.

"Gather 'round. I want to know what each of you has been doing since I saw you last. I miss you so, each of you. You must tell me everything about everything—and don't skip a luscious gory detail. I simply have to know."

She passes another plate of cookies, so for a moment our mouths are too stuffed to begin to speak. She begins easily enough,

"Cat got your tongues? Bashful? Well, then, I'll go first and we'll listen to each of you later. Let's see, of course you remember the Diamond Ball last fall. I was gorgeous. Silver lamé gown fit me like the finger of a glove, silver fox stole, silver bag looked like a bulging bunch of grapes, tiara with radiating silver feathers like a holy halo in one of those old religious pictures, and silver sandals with four inch heels. Three princes and an ambassador danced with me, but only one movie star. All the other women hated me, I could tell. They glared. I know they were jealous. My picture was in the paper, sitting beside Marvin Davis. Of course you heard about the police coming–that was in the paper too. Hunter S. Thompson became disruptive, tried to paw me when he had dragged me onto the dance floor. I swung my purse at him, and the clang was so loud it got everyone's attention. I don't know if it was the clang of the purse or the clang of his head, but my purse was deeply dented, and I am suing him for the damages. It was pretty well repaired at the auto body shop, it is true, but it is the principle of the thing–I am a toad of high principle. And one of the princes keeps calling and sending flowers, but I don't think he's a real prince. On the other hand, who cares as long as he is as wealthy as he seems? I think he is an ex-Nazi, but he's nice. And, oh, so many exciting things are happening. I may be receiving my honorary doctorate in laws as an indirect result of some favors I did a Supreme Court judge. My cookie recipe won honorable mention at the county fair. I have been invited to the Philippines for a women's conference because I am definitely the most feminine and liberated toad in the hemisphere. And the affairs and the invitations and the honors are all so much . . . so I did something just for me. I purchased (on credit) this unique and spacious caravan wagon. The color is 'special order' to go with my outfit. The horse is a thoroughbred Japanese Kobe, locked in a closet and fattened force-fed on beer. And inside" (she histrionically gesticulates) "a kitchen complete with microwave and dishwasher, a television lounge with tilt seating, a compact but thorough bathroom with hot water and a small Jacuzzi, and heated water beds for six (not to forget the horse) . . . and what else could anyone desire? So let us embark on a journey beyond anyone's wildest dreams. First to the showers is muddy little Moley. And, Ratty, come. If you are too lazy, then, we'll carry you. Badger, you're the only other woman here. Come, help me in the kitchen. Can you make a pie crust? Mine often is so heavy. Kenneth, Kenneth, I have so been looking forward to our chance to chat . . . but not now. Maybe later . . ."

And she is a whirlwind whirling, and the wagon wheels are rolling, and she didn't hear our stories. She isn't a good listener. Toady is more a producer-director, a whirlwind in the aspens.

9. Rattling And Lurching

Crashing down the mountain on this huge wagon, I ride the brake and rein as delicately as I can my best guesses to the horse Oliver, I sitting so much higher than he (and often almost lose my footing . . . er, my seating). We work together as well as any two might do who have never worked together before and who are so distant in species and language. The last time I crashed down this absence of road I was crazed and my feet were nimble. Now I am calmly sane, and it is the weight of this vehicle which bears us down, and the width of this vehicle which slows us up catching on bushes and saplings. Neither Oliver nor I knows how we can avoid a rumble-booming splintering destruction, and I can see in my mind's eye the final shreds of wagon, equipment and beloved folk skittering down the scree, bodies rolling, loose wheels wobbling, sticks of wood and a bird cage end over end over end until inertia and gravity settle their slow arm wrestling match. I think of injured Ratty inside on a waterbed strapped down, but since I cannot hear him screaming through the rumble of the bouncing wheels and squeaking chassis' syncopated percussion against the trees, I let it roll on, and don't let on I am not the one who is guiding this barge, and Oliver nods at me and neighs, as if to say neither is it he.

Rattling and lurching all day has left me staggering and vibrating when we stop by the river to make our camp before the sun goes down. I don't know how she does it, but Toady has spent the day cooking in that tossing, jumping chamber now stilled beneath the trees, and her soufflé has not fallen. We eat as never in our lives: fresh breads, cheeses, pickled beets, pickled baby corn, pickled baby, artichokes, potted salmon, potted lobster, paté of snake and hare, deviled quail eggs, heavenly hash, bird's nest soup, roast of buffalo, green beans, wax beans, lima beans, pinto beans, black beans, mung beans, garbanzo beans, jelly beans, shredded potatoes with shredded coconut and shredded lime rind, boiled new potatoes with parsley, baked potatoes with crunchy fried ants, whipped potatoes with white gravy and wrinkled raisins, hazel nut soufflé eels in aspic, lady fingers, angel cake, devil's food cake, sponge cake with lychees, pound cake with pomegranate jelly, and home made persimmon ice cream.

After dinner we dance wildly around the campfire, and only slightly in it (but I wasn't badly burnt), and even Ratty sits with us and shakes his uninjured finger in time with our music. What a mixture of sights and fears and tastes and excitements it has been! We finally fall panting around the spindle of his shaking finger, we sweaty jellyfish, all stiffness melted from our bones.

"Oh, Kenneth, you dance divinely."

"Thank you, Monica my dear. You exaggerate, as usual, and you flatter, but despite my recent love affair with truth I accept your compliment, and without exaggeration or flattery I tell you flatly honestly you are one hell of a toad."

"It is my mission in life to keep things lively, and I never tire of it. What is it you do, Kenneth?"

"I used to know. I was a banker. I wrote for fun, because I wanted to. Perhaps the writing saved me from catastrophe, but not completely. I came to my personal crisis inevitably, probably in the wake of the death of my son. Mad, I sought the boy in me, which has brought me to some different ways of feeling, thinking, acting. I am only somewhere along the way, and it is anything but easy, yet I live each day, each moment—and my life brings me here with you. I rejoice in each of you, but do I know you at all?"

"You know us, Kenneth. As you share with us you know us better every day."

"We know you, Kenneth, but our knowledge only comes from not having to hide, not having to disremember. Your knowledge comes from progressive discovery."

"Thank you, Ratty. You state it clearly. I think I understand."

"Even I know who we are together. I can feel it, and I remember from the beginning. I can't explain it all, but I can know. Mostly I know when I am alone I am afraid and silent, and when I am with Ratty I feel confident because I understand things, and when I am with Badger I know I can act right, and when I am with Toady I can play and dance and laugh and eat . . ."

"I hear the wisdom of our quiet little Mole. Each of us is identifiably separate—Rat to scrutinize sharply, to analyze; Mole to feel, to respond with honest emotion; Badger to protect with loyalty and moral sense; Toad to have appetite and impulse and flair, a source of energy; and I . . . what have I to offer to this partnership?"

"Oh, Kenneth, you are the author. You pull us together."

"But I do nothing like that any more. When I was Director I thought I accomplished a great deal, but when I got sick the bank went on without me and I felt empty. Now I accept my life passively, do only what is before me, what is in this moment, the path of least resistance. No longer can I attack the problems of life and the world. No longer can I seek success or wealth or fame. By my old standards I am a weakling. How can I hold us together?"

"Do you really feel like a weakling, you fantastic John Travolta of a dancer?"

"Do you feel unwise or morally weak, you who have brought us together here, who have led us almost unscathed through a most horrid storm?"

"Do you feel dull and imperspicuous, you who have helped me understand Aristotle and the trigonometry of felling trees?"

"Can you feel unfeeling, you who sought me where I was lost, with every kind of love, through every kind of fear?"

Our quiet discussion of who we are and why integrates itself with a night of joyful energetic dreaming through all the meaning of all the day, from the top of the massive mountain to the middle, the trauma and the feast, the conversation and the discovery, and more to come each morrow.

10. Knotted Self

Our second day down the mountain is not so steep. Oliver and I continue our partnership in weaving a road out of what is not a road, but as our way becomes a little less vertical, and as we make our way on the outside or the inside of the trees along the riverbank (my job to guess which way will work) we progress down the mountain with our precious cargo of my four closest friends: Ratty really healing despite the rough ride; Badger making lunch or darning socks; Monica Toad doing her nails; and little Moley jumping from one bed to another, one bench to another, peeking around the edges of the windows on the lookout for savage Caucasians, occasionally poofing one away with his tranquilizer blow gun.

I ride along high in the driver's box and remember the important parts of my previous journey down this path. It is as if I had been juggling the deadly franticness of the life I had been forced to abandon, the confidence and serenity I knew existed for me but I had barely touched, and the compulsion to find the boy I had never known. It all added up to the same thing, I guess, an attempt to stay alive with no idea of what my life means. Now I laugh a little, because I am a bit different. For me now it makes little sense to try to stay alive, or to try to do anything. That sounds strange in light of my old assumptions, but now I have no assumptions in particular, and I am certainly more free. Free for what? (I wonder to myself). Free to be here, now (I answer me). I tied myself in knots with assumptions, and tied knots about my knotted self with assumptions. And what did the assumptions add up to? (I ask myself again, rhetorically). I'm not sure I know (I cautiously consider to myself evasively, somewhat bored with the attitude with which I have been treating myself in this conversation). The assumptions add up to wanting to please Mommy and Daddy, and by extension and extension and extension trying to please everyone in the world, to be handsome, to be rich, to be powerful, to be helpful, to be intelligent, to be perfect . . . but not to be, not to be myself, not to be free. I don't know how to quantify this freedom or this being me, nor could I wish to. I don't have to call it good or bad in whole or part. It is mine to live, and I would be foolish to abandon my beloved unknown life. And I am tiring of this tedious analytic consideration of the ineffable, unless it is really important to you (I assert to myself politely).

And the sunshine, and the dapples of shadow beneath the deciduous trees along the river, and the arrhythmical clunking of the wheels and the wagon, and the simple songs of birds, and Oliver's snorts, and all the other temperatures and colors and vibrations in the entire universe . . . these are pleasant to this empty-minded bouncer on this barge floating down the swollen river to the prairie. I have no other need this moment than to be here, floating to there.

I am driving the wagon, but our anxious Toad is driving all of us. She has asked me many times (but I don't know how many, since I don't count things any more) how far it is to Avalon, How long it will take us to get there. I haven't even been tempted to make up an answer because, simply, I do not know. I am willing to try to estimate . . . Let me see . . . Perhaps we are halfway down the mountain, and perhaps the foothills and the flatlands are still where they were . . . but I don't remember how far it may be to the city, if they haven't moved it, if it exists, if it ever existed.

11. What I Want

"You are an infuriating man!"

"Which is the pejorative, 'infuriating' or 'man'?"

"Ohhh! (blb blb) you are an infuriating man!"

"You understand, Toady, I have told you what I know, although it is not what you have wanted to hear."

"I only want what I want. Why does everyone obstruct me?"

"I do not obstruct you, nor would I wish to. I am helping you down the mountain, even though for myself, I could stay here forever."

"Well, I don't want to stay in the wilderness. It's good enough for a day, but I have been there three. I want back in the city where there is life, action. And I have things to do, which is something you used to understand, but now I don't know about you."

"I don't know about me either, thought I did, never did. As to the city, if we need to get there we will get there, without trying too very hard. As to your projects, Toady, they usually get us in some sort of trouble, but we usually go along with you because we love you immeasurably. You are a part of us. But don't get me wrong–I don't think any of us approves of what cannot be approved. We may give you leeway (as if we had any choice about it) but we each will make up our own minds about what we want."

"I know what I want–the last cassowary."

12. Whispers

Camp by the river tonight is subdued. No raucous singing, no frenzied dancing. Badger has cooked a hearty healthy meal of stew and cornbread. We eat in silence, but after supper unheard whispers flit about like clouds of gnats.

"She wants what?"

"The last cassowary."

"She wants what?"

"The last cassowary."

"I heard that, but what is a cassowary?"

"It's a bird."

"She wants a what?"

"I thought you said you heard me."

"I heard you, but . . . a bird?'

"It's a big bird."

"Why does she want the last cassowary?"

"I don't know."

"The last cassowary?"

"I guess so. She said so."

"Is it the last cassowary?"

"I don't know."

"Isn't there another cassowary?'

"I don't know."

"I mean, can't there be a cassowary for Toady?"

"I don't know."

"What does she want to do with a cassowary?"

"I don't know."

"Maybe she wants it for a pet."

"I doubt it."

"Couldn't she want it for a pet?"

"Can you imagine Toady taking care of a pet?"

"But a little bird in a cage . . ."

"Four feet tall, twenty stone and able to eviscerate a man in one kick."

"Large cage?"

"No cage. No pet."

"Feathers?"

"Feathers."

"Oh, no."

"I'm afraid so, or something like it."

"How can we stop her?"

"Have you ever stopped her doing anything?"

"I can't stop her. Maybe all of us together . . ."

"I don't think so. We can't flip switches in her head. We can't lock her up or tie her down. We've tried that before. It doesn't work."

"We can't let her do this, but we can't stop her from doing this. What can we do?"

"We can get some sleep. We are not at the city yet. Something will happen . . . a broken axle, a snowstorm, a migration of cassowaries . . . anything but . . ."

". . . anything but a change of heart or mind. Our Toady is a gem, obdurate as a diamond."

13. Species And Subspecies

Our third day out of the meadow brings us to the foothills as I had expected, but even before our view of the flatlands was clear, I sensed something I did not expect. It was an uneasy sense, vague, momentary but lasting, like the distant not yet identifiable scent when driving the car over the road fast, and I find myself sniffing. "Something . . ." I say, but I can't quite find it. In a moment I say, "Skunk!" and hold my breath through the intense part, see the poor animal's carcass in the road, swerve not to hit it (for if it touches the car we will smell it the rest of the trip), and the odor abates as we speed away. And we always comment how intense and distinct it is, this phenomenon we avoid.

And that moment ago when I had a sensation, it was as if I stood on the jutting red rocks at the edge of the vast dry ancient ocean and saw the flatlands teeming with dinosaurs, an extensive swamp unbelievably roaring and writhing with reptiles ripping one another, nipping pieces and running, screaming in terror and terribleness. Even though it was a mere vision, I thought of these animals (souled beings) whom I had romanticized as a small child, whose species and subspecies I had memorized as my way to master what is terrifying. My psyche instructed me to master dinosaurs, so I thought it was my own idea, my unique experience.

I was surprised to find other children doing the same. It never occurred to me until that moment ago that all the dinosaur books and toys and posters I cherished were purposely made and sold by the millions exactly for children like me. And it never occurred to me until this very moment to wonder if what seemed my own unique psychic existential experience was more determined by the biology of being a child or by the arbitrary commercial lusts of book and toy marketers.

And now I do stand on this ancient prominence and I see exactly what my vision saw—the entire valley below me now filled with exact squares, dull and flat, each exactly alongside and aligned with four others, each exactly touching its corners with four others, quadrangular crystals, a growing mold, algae overfilling a stagnant swamp. The heedless mindless suburbs are attacking the mountains.

I wish to go back. In the mountains I am at one with "I am who I am" because even though I do not know who I am, I know I do not know who I am. In the city I don't know anything, but I think I do. There are millions of my species, and I don't know who any of them is.

> "Are you going to stand there all day gaping, or are you going to get on the wagon and drive? You act like some mountain hermit who never saw civilization. Come on, Kenneth, get with it."

> "Oh, Monica. I was just thinking."

> "I don't pay you to think."

"You don't pay me."

"I was just joking."

"All jokes are serious at some level."

14. Hot Dogs

The wagon is slower than the automobiles, and much broader. Without exception they honk angrily as they swerve past. Poor Oliver, stolid though he is, must be hurt or frightened by the noise, the threats, the wincing closeness of the passes and the piercing coldness of the hatred. It seems simple to me to acknowledge the reality this is a horse-drawn wagon and is likely to act like one, but it must seem to them it is something in their way, that all objects must accommodate their directions, speeds and expectations. I hope God protects the Amish from such abuse.

The wagon is much faster on the flat pavement than it was lurching through the pathless forest, the rocky riverbank. Toady is excited and wants to be in the city "now!", but she contains herself better than I would have guessed, does not abuse Oliver or me, good-humoredly waves at the opaque tinted windows of the passing cars with her dainty lace handkerchief, smiles broadly, squeaks her unheard falsetto jokes, "Rhett Butler, Ah do declare." and "Prince Pribilof, how charmed I am to see you again."

It has been a long morning coming from the mountainside at daybreak. As long as we are in civilization we may as well take advantage of it, we opine. It is easier to stop a slow wagon than it is to stop a speeding car. In the wagon it is easy not to miss the Denny's. Moley is especially excited (and always hungry) because he has heard of hot dogs but cannot remember having eaten one.

"Do they have hot dogs at this restaurant? Do they? Do they?"

"Yes, Moley, I am sure they do."

"Do they really cook dogs?"

"No, Moley, I am sure they do not."

"Well, then what is a hot dog?"

"A hot dog is a sausage filled with questionable matter and salt."

"Will I like it?"

"Probably, Moley. Most children do."

"Are the rest rooms clean in these places?"

"Toady, I hear their motto is 'So clean you can eat off the floor'."

"Are you joking?"

"Of course I'm joking. (But jokes are always serious, at some level.)"

We five go into Denny's. We thought of bringing Oliver with us, but leave him tied outside with his feed bag. We thought they might not allow animals inside.

"Seat Yourself", so we do. We peruse the menus. They do have hot dogs, and several pages more of attractive pictures. I remember for a moment that I used to eat in restaurants frequently. Maitres d' all knew me. I over-tipped. I expected recognition. They knew that. I got recognition in proportion as they got over-tipped. Now I wonder what they really thought of me, a self-important puffed up toad.

> "The trout looks good. I used to get trout right out of the river. Yes, trout is good for a badger."

> "I believe I will have a cheese omelet. Cheese is good for this rat."

> "I'll probably have pancakes, a mountain man's favorite."

> "I don't know exactly what to order. I don't see anything quite elegant enough for me. Let me think . . . What's most expensive?"

> "Stop thinking and get me a hot dog. I'm ready."

The waitress approaches, and we are all ready.

> "I'm sorry, Sir, but you will have to leave your animals outside. (And for a moment I thought that would apply to you, too, you look so much like a bear from back there, so rugged, and all that hair.)"

> "My what?"

"Animals are not allowed in restaurants."

"These are my friends, my companions."

"I'm sure they are. Do you want me to call the manager?"

"We just want to get something to eat . . ."

"What seems to be the problem here?"

"This (ungentle) man refuses to take his animals out."

"You must not bring animals into a food establishment. It's the law. Only seeing-eye dogs are allowed."

"Well then, it's alright because these are my feeling-heart mole, my thinking-brain rat, my enjoying-life toad and my trusting-conscience badger. Can we order now?"

"Shall I call the police?"

"No, we are leaving."

"But, my hot dog!"

"I'd say I'm sorry, Moley, that you don't get to eat your first hot dog, but I am not sorry—hot dogs are vile. Let's go eat in the wagon, with good old Oliver. We'll get by, together. I guess Denny will have to eat the hot dogs."

15. This Tragedy

Again to Avalon. The way is familiar, and I am afraid. After our stop at a roadside park we are enough rested and enough fed. Now the highway is easy to roll along lazy. Oliver clops along humming to himself, and I have little to do but sit and wish him well. I have something dangerous to do, I am afraid. I have to think.

I was in Avalon twice: the first fifteen years of my life for one, and the day last autumn when I came to find my inner child, found him, was killed and died. It is hard for me to wonder what the third visit to this city will bring, for I fear it.

I wish to be on the mountain. I was there three times: most recently the winter I survived alone and not alone, not long before that the initiation of my journey seeking the boy, and necessarily by logic (but missing from my memory) an earlier being-there which allowed me to recognize the meadow.

I have lived in several personae during the past months: the madness of a manic man who had worked for decades to change the world, which changed despite him, changes always; the frantic hot and cold of the pilgrim in search of himself, losing himself searching; the isolation of the hermit at the very edge, who in ceasing seeking finds surrender is not the same as dependency; and here I am with my newly met ancient familiars, my "family" in fact entering this city, society in all its threatening aspects.

Whom do I love? From the beginning, and briefly: I do not consider my family because I left them behind so long ago; I cannot consider my wives because they used me, did not love me truly; I believe I love my children, but they have been withheld from me so we have shared little, and I suspect my love for them is a kind of sentimentality (I wish I could do better.); and these fantastic friends!–among them I am whole.

What sorts of relationships have I had? It is too easy to blame myself for being blind and selfish. I ask in order to wonder how I can live better now. I am willing to be willing. Perhaps it is hidden dependency which is the most destructive, secret agendas I am the last to know, which almost always attract someone whose blind unrealistic expectations exactly fit with my own. It is not at all only sexual. I have had minor and major disasters with teachers, business partners, customers, neighbors, friends, political enemies, bureaucrats, entire bureaucracies, clergymen every bit as much as with wives and women who wished to be wives. Blind and selfish, that's what we usually are. We can't know it because we can't see it, and so we can't change it.

How can this come about? I remember I vowed to be a good parent long before I had a child. (I wonder why.) I tried to be a good parent to my children. I felt an overwhelming need to care for the boy, once I felt he existed, was mine and I didn't know him. I find it easy to act as a kind parent toward little Moley. What is so important about being a good parent? It is the quiet joy of being able to say, "That must hurt a lot." instead of, "There, there, don't cry."

A little seed of honesty, plant a little seed of honesty before society shellacs over the little heart another layer every day. No wonder we get plastered regularly–we have to cover over any little truth which might leak out of our little hearts inside. That's what happened to me–I cracked open just before I died, went screaming down the mountain looking for my little truth, the little boy I was.

Did I say I didn't care about the family I grew up in? I must! My heart is opening now, melting in the understanding that all the little children, every one was covered over, overlooked. Whether we knew it or not, we had to cover our true selves over over and over, coming and going–not like the overcoats we had to put on going out only and only in the winter, but emotional armor rigid going out into the world and coming back into the family also.

Everyone I know has suffered this tragedy of childhood. I have never met a "normal" person, just a lot of actors. That is something I love about Badger, that I know she suffered, but somehow she became liberated from dishonesty. I think she still wears the armor, but she knows what's under it, can take it off. Mine was welded shut. It took life-threatening death to shatter it. I don't want it back, not even stainless steel shorts and tank top. Like a two year old, I like life naked. No diapers, no armor. I'm headed out to play in the snow.

Everyone I know has suffered this tragedy of childhood. That means my parents! They have suffered the same, each in her and his own ways. And my father's father, and my mother's mother. And my ugly successful brother, and my ugly unsuccessful brother. The child lives because the child feels. My dead father lives not as the man he acted but as the child he felt.

This is helping, but what is this helping? Rolling down the road to Avalon.

16. Excited

"There's the city. Look out the window to your right."

"I can't see anything."

"Your other right, Moley."

"Oh, I see it. I see it! I see it! Toady, look. No, Toady, over here, the other right. Ratty, look. It's the city!"

"Wonderful,   wonderful,   wonderful, wonderful . . . We'll be at Toad Hall in an hour, loudly won't we, Oliver?"

"Neigh."

"Well, an hour and a half, then . . . and do I have some things to do, and some surprises for all of you. You know I love you, and there is nothing I wouldn't do for you. I only think of you, my dearest friends, don't I?"

"Not always, Toady."

"hummphrrummph"

". . . But often."

"Yes. I do you many favors and you love me."

"We do love you."

"I was thinking about when I was last here."

"I was here for three years in the university and never left the campus, then I left the campus and went to my garret and never left my garret."

"Oh, Ratty, go back to reading your Aristotle. That book is just the size for your head."

"When were you in Avalon last, Badger?"

"I have never been to the city. In all my long life I have never been to the city . . . and Boy! am I excited."

"You have never been to the city, Badger?"

"Never, but now is the time, and I'm going to see everything and do everything, and I may even go dancing until the sun comes up, and I am going to buy a bonnet and an apron and oranges and licorice and . . ."

"Hey, Ratty. Get your head out of that book and help Badger make a list. She'll never remember these things on her own."

"Badger, you are the greatest old friend ever. I'll go dancing with you, just like we did before, but I have to be in bed by nine o'clock. I'll help you go shopping, too. Ratty, please put a toy on the shopping list. Okay, Ratty?"

"Oh, Moley, I'll get you a toy myself, just because I love you."

"Me too."

"And I."

"And put it on my list, young Mister Rat."

"Wow! How many toys is that, Ratty?"

"Just the right number, my little friend."

"Just the right everything. I'm glad to be with each and all of you. My family, I love you."

"Okay, Oliver, I'm in the box now. Let's get with it. Toad Hall in ten minutes! Okay, twenty . . . but pick it up the best you can. I have work to do."

17. A Moment Is The Pivot

Square city gradually gets familiar with me. Slow drag of Main shows bits and persons. This is the way to travel, a yellow wagon trimmed in red and green. Even city people come out of their holes to stare. If you wave bravely and openly at them, they timidly finger-wiggle back, squeak "Hi". I had seen the sterility of the city's plans, overlooked that there might be living little crabs in these hollow-looking shells. I feel more alive now than I did a moment ago, because if they are alive a little, I am too.

And it is so, gloriously for each of us, that a moment is the pivot. One moment I am afraid, and because clarity comes to bless me the next moment I am at peace. And each moment in the flow of reality in its infinite directions is the pivot upon which swivels the entire universe. And each moment is my opportunity to let me loose and spin around the All of the universe as if it were a Hershey's kiss, and I can be so great because I am so small. This may be a big old hollow shell I live in, but because I am so insignificantly small I can afford to live here and grow and grow and grow and live and cry and hug you for understanding why I am spinning around the universe as if I had just been kissed by a whole smiling sunny sandy beach full of little mean city people and a big piece of chocolate.

Rolling down the streets becomes a rhythmic song, and sitting in the coach now I am not alone. Moley and I look out the window, gape and wave. Badger knits smiling. Ratty closes Aristotle, shares our window on the world, probably a little bit to compete with me, mostly to share with me being with Moley, discovering the world with him. I become aware how much Ratty, despite what seems to me his youth, has already closed himself off from the outside, his rational haughtiness incompletely covering naked fear.

We come to venerable Toad Hall, a red brick Georgian mansion imperfectly elegant, morally larger than Toady herself, older, contributed into by her progenitors. Toad Hall is spacious altogether, but many of her rooms are smaller chambers than would be made today. She is solid, but her covered over cracks are real, results of strains at this tiny segment of the surface of the stolid earth much bigger than a house. The furnishings also are beyond Miss Toady's whims. She dare not remove tapestries or family portraits, cracking leather sofas or delicate Louis Quatorze chairs. When she installed a hot tub, she had to save the old claw-footed deep enameled iron one as a planter on the veranda. I guess she does not resent so much that she cannot destroy the house, but that she is secretly comforted that it is too big and old for her to change, that it is what can contain her own explosive self, keep her safe from her own impulses (somewhat), that the house belongs to her as an epitome of all who came before her, contributed to her being who she is. Toad Hall understands Monica Toad, comforts her, protects her, gives her identity. It is her home.

18. Make Yourselves At Home

"Make yourselves at home. I have some things to do. I shall return later."

"Aren't you tired, Toad? We have been travelling for days. We have been looking forward to getting here, resting together for a while. Why are you in such a hurry?"

"That is exactly what I am doing. I am just getting something we need for our homecoming."

"Is this the book you mean, Toady?"

"Yes, Ratty. You can use the desk in the library. Remember, when you make the list, only those with a check mark and a star. Do not include any with a question mark. Oh, yes, also do not include any marked with a capital D. They're dead . . . er, I mean deceased. Yes, 'D' means deceased."

"I tried to feed Oliver, Toady dear, as you said to, but he just snorted and pulled straw over his head. I think he's going to take a nap. I think his snorts meant, 'I'm not going to the store.'"

"That's okay, Moley baby. You'll help me do the marketing when I return from my errand. The super markets are open twenty-four hours in the city."

"Toady, dear, the kitchen is clean. I have taken the china from the basement, as you requested, and I have washed every dish in the dishwasher. What a machine! Who would have thought you could put dozens of dishes in a box, close the door, turn a knob, wait half an hour, and have all the dishes cleaned and dried? You have a wonderful kitchen. And that large oven! I have never seen one so large. I think you could roast an ostrich in there."

"Toady, what are you up to?"

"Oh, Kenneth, don't worry. I'm just arranging a little homecoming supper for us. Give me some space now, I have things to do."

"You were going to have Oliver haul a lot of stuff from the market, but he is an animal and too smart, or too honest, to fall for it. He's tired. We're all tired. You should be tired. You have hooked Ratty and Moley and even level-headed Badger into doing tasks for your project, while you direct the world around you according to your own wishes, your own impulses, your own appetites. I love you. Even though I, too, am tired, I will try to help. What is your errand now? Where are you going?'

"Do you think you can handle my big four-wheel drive, the one with the winch? And how good a cowboy are you, Kenneth? Can you use a lasso?"

19. The Last Cassowary

"Swan Lake?"

"Just do what I tell you to. I know he's here. He has to be here. I hope he's here. They said he was still here . . ."

And I see the most amazing little thing I have ever seen. I see a few swans, and hundreds of white ducks in droves, making tidal waves toward whatever part of the chain-link fence is contacted on the other side by humans, sources of bread. And among the ducks, part of the middle of each wave, a larger white feathered thing meant to be hidden in the flock. It is huge, fully four feet tall. Its lower extremities are long and massive. Its wings are insignificant flippers. Its head is like a large stone, not much beak protruding from it in proportion to its circumference, almost as big around as a small duck. But what is striking is that I have been unobservant enough, even for a moment, to perceive this as part of the flock, not to notice this glaring misfit whose efforts at camouflage are too poor to be laughable. The white feathers, stuck on with duck spit, are falling like rose petals a week after the prom. The few white feathers which remain are there by Brownian laws, not by mucilage. Dark feathers over the melon-shaped body show, and especially brilliant yellow and blue about the face. And it wrenches my heart to see this feathered biped arduously ducking, making like a duck.

"The last cassowary?"

"The very last."

"Pitiful, isn't it?"

"Beautiful, don't you think?"

"Yes, but not for the same reasons you do, I fear."

"I don't think this will be too difficult, if you can just get the lasso around his neck."

"I don't agree with you."

"Oh. Worried about the other people calling the police? Forget it. No problem. No one wants to get involved in anything any more. There isn't a chance in a thousand any of them will cause us any trouble, and if they look like they're going to, I'll just tell them we are with the Humane Society. Didn't you see the sticker I put on the side of the car? 'Avalon Humane Society' Real professional looking, huh?"

"Toady, why are you doing this? We've given it some thought, and we know you're not interested in the welfare of this tragic bird."

"No, I'm doing this for you. Come on, get your rope. Let's go before it starts to get dark."

"No, Toady, not until you tell me honestly what your motivation is. As much as I care about this animal, I love you better. I want to know what this means to you."

"Come on, Kenneth. You're wasting my time. Just trust me. This is important. Get the rope."

"No, Toady. Tell me what it is you are trying to do for me or us. Maybe it isn't what we want or need."

"Oh, okay, if you really must know. Ratty is inviting the crème de la crème for a formal dinner party at Toad Hall tomorrow night, in your honor. Only the best will be there (I put a 'D' by Hunter Thompson's name). Moley is helping me, and Badger is supervising all the servants in the kitchen, but we just want you to be the guest of honor. Now, aren't you ashamed of giving me such a hard time?"

"No. I am not ashamed, and I do not accept your answer. You have told me neither why you want to capture this animal, nor what is in it for you. I want to know now."

"You are an infuriating man! Okay, look. No one in this jerkwater town—absolutely no one—has ever eaten roast of cassowary. It will make your homecoming dinner the affair of the year, the affair of the decade. You will be famous around here. It will be written up in the newspapers!"

"I am afraid to meet even one person, and she wants to make me famous. Toady, I love you and I want you to love me, but I do not want a formal dinner, and I do not want roast of cassowary. I really don't."

"I don't know where your priorities are. I don't think you have any sense. I don't think you know what's good for you. I think you are ungrateful! Who are you to decline to accept such a great thing I offer you? Who do you think you are?"

"The last whatever-I-am."

"What kind of a friend would frustrate my dearest dreams? Don't you know how much I want to do all this, for you?"

"Somehow I don't get the impression it is for me. I know it isn't for the cassowary. What is it you really want, Toady?"

"The yellow and blue feathers will make a lovely hat, the exact colors of my new outfit."

"That makes sense. It is a relief to know my dear self-centered Toad is just as fatuous as ever. And it is a touching joy to see the last cassowary dodging like a duck, trying to quack, trying to stay alive. Let's go home now."

20. A Wonderful Banquet

We have a wonderful banquet. The table is full enough just with the five of us. The table is elegant enough just with the flowers Moley has brought from the garden. The board is laid just sumptuously enough with the simple food Badger has prepared: green salad, hot breads, fresh vegetable soup, pan-fried trout rolled in corn meal, boiled new potatoes, carrots candied without too much brown sugar, blackberry pie and raspberry leaf and maple bark tea. Decorum is just subdued enough with Toady quietly moping at her end of the table hatless. Toasting is just erudite enough with Ratty setting the tone, terse, honest and perceptive.

"With this aromatic tea I toast Us. No friends are truer because no friends are honester. We withhold nothing from one another, nor do we impose on each other what has no meaning. Each of us tries to live each day, each moment, for what it is to us, and we try to bring to it something of who we are inside. It seems too easy in society to conveniently conventionally hide true feelings, true motives, true life behind the fixed grin of a mask. We do our smiling more straightforwardly—exactly at the moment when we feel the smile we share it with each other. We do not evade or avert what is not laughing or smiling. We express as freely what some call darker feelings. I propose a toast to Toady, grumping like a silent cloud reluctant to drop her hurt and angry tears. She shows what I have said—we are not saints, but we are thoroughly honest. To Toady!"

"Oh, you foolish wise little Rat! I wanted to be too stingy to cry in front of all of you, and now you have me crying—see, the tears are ruining my makeup, and I don't care—and you have me laughing through my tears. I love you, Ratty. I love all of you. I love you more than my picture in the paper or a new hat."

"Now I toast our little Mole. No one is more honest than the true perennial child. Some call him simple, but the truth is simple. How un-simple he is is reflected in our love for him, its innumerable facets. Among the others of us is sophistication, experience, suffering, confusion, but we look to Moley for simplicity, the true resonance of the soul with what is here and now, pure tones without confusing undertones and overtones. Perhaps his is the tonic of our communal symphony."

"I don't understand a word you say, dear Rat, but I understand all you say, and I am proud you love me—almost as proud as I am that you can say so many words."

"To Mole!"

"Hooray! Hooray! (and hugs and kisses)."

"Beloved Badger, you have cared for us from before the beginning. Almost always you express your care in quiet action, doing what is needful. Your words are few, and usually pessimistic, cautious. When we see you in the kitchen reading the newspaper we know you are quietly making a count of the lives lost on the first page. (What a way to start a morning!) Your wisdom is deep, practical, drawn from knowledge of hard knocks in the world, molded as a useful tool and a beautiful sculpture from you own suffering. This dinner is delicious. Thank you. You are delicious, a flavor each of carries which makes palatable the bitter moments in our lives. We toast you, Badger."

"And our guest of honor, Kenneth. Don't you know how important you are? Just because you have been doing some housecleaning recently as an isolated hermit, have you forgotten how important you are to us and many others? Just because you learned you have to be able to live with yourself, don't you know you can live with others, too? Because you are better able to live with yourself you are better able to live in the world of living persons. Just because you have learned you are imperfect, sometimes foolish, even dangerous, you are more able to live in the real human world with danger, falsity and injustice. You were dancing clumsily with death, and now you know how sweet life is each moment. We love you, Kenneth, just for living your life. We think you wise and brave and kind to do it. We identify with you, and wish you well now."

"Hear, hear! Hip, hip! Hooray for Kenneth!"

"My idea of a real man."

"I feel safe with you, Kenneth."

"I am proud of you."

"Let us have a speech from you, Kenneth, to cap your going-away banquet. Maybe it will be in the newspapers. I will take notes."

"I think I'm beginning to understand. From the beginning of my metamorphosis I have become increasingly alive. When I was crazy I was becoming wise. When I was killed I was becoming alive. When I was utterly isolated I was coming to be lovable, perhaps someday to be loved. And when you all came together with me, I was already loved, and will be as long as I live. Among you is the love I was born into and the love I carry with me, previously hidden. It is you I carry with me. Even though each of you may have her or his own life, to me you have some special meanings I carry with me now, forever. Mole, you show me I have feelings–I had tried to forget. Toad, you show me I am egotistical, but also that can bring joy, and singing and dancing. Badger, you show me I carry within me the calm and the wisdom to care for myself, that no catastrophe is news, that I can survive, and if I don't the world won't come to an end just because

I have. And Rat, beautiful dark lad, you rodent Kierkegaard, you remind me of my energy when I was omnipotent, omniscient—an adolescent. Discoveries and insights and friendships were weighty for me then, and are again, and will be. I love you each and all. I know you better now than I had before. Come to me now, all together. Let us hug close, and when we let go we will not lose each other. I carry you with me in my heart."

And Toad Hall is gone, and my friends. And I am warm, full, unafraid—in the middle of the city.

LEARNING TO LISTEN,
LISTENING TO LEARN

1. I Walk

There is a way. I do not know it, you may not know it. Authorities and experts do not know the way. I do not learn the way by defying authorities (although it is easy to prove to myself they are wrong). Enough pain and enough failure have taught me I have been wrong. I cannot be right right now if I was wrong a while ago. All I have changed is my self-righteousness. Can that be enough? To learn I have been wrong has confronted me with impenetrable dark clouds of guilt and shame within which I have nearly perished. However, I have been learning day by day—I have been learning I am a living thing who needs to be cared for, and I have been learning I carry within me capacities to care for me, and I have been learning others care for me as much as I am available to be cared for, and I have been learning I cannot rule the world, nor can I change it—and I can continue learning as long as I do not impose old ideas which expect me already to know everything and already to have everything and already to be everything.

Aristotle's teacher Plato said his own teacher Socrates said, "I know that I do not know," (but I do not know where he said it). So, my beloved Greek friends have suggested to me one pivotal conviction, that my ignorance is useful. A start.

I don't know this city any more. It has grown beyond what I once understood. I know of myself only that I am, that I have nothing more than me. All my past I carry with me somehow, but it ain't negotiable.

I am hungry. I can walk, but I can't walk into a restaurant or a grocery store. I can walk and see what I learn, learn what I see.

To the center. It is a pleasant morning. I walk. I experiment with walking. I shuffle—too much friction on my shoes. I hop—too much pounding to my knees. I stride, make each step take as much of the pavement as it can. I stand me so erect I arch back some. I stride. I take my chin off my chest, arch my back, raise my head and stride. I look about and see each house is different, each person whom I see is different from each other. Without cataloguing them I let it be recorded in me I have seen them. Still, I am myself striding to the center of the city, not asking anyone to have anything to do with me, just getting used to being open enough myself to see them. You see, before, I think I was blind so I saw little of what was before me. Now I wish to see, and far deeper than my eyes is where are sketched the traces of my seeing you, seeing the old lady on the porch with her cat, the twelve year old on his glowing green skateboard across the street, the aproned Asian sweeping before his store whose signs I can not read despite the care with which they were lettered, the letter carrier attending to her work . . . Each automobile which passes me leaves its traces, even though I cannot tell you each model and color, how it sounded, where it turned, where it was going, the license plate number. Most amazing to me is that I do not see passing automobiles as machines, or even as animated machines, but I am convinced in each of them is a person driving, that that person's personality likely had to do with the choosing of that car, that that person's personality and behavior have something to do with the sounds and speeds and directions and turnings and honkings and radio noises and choices of stations . . .

Aristotle told me there were things which grew by nature, and there were things which followed different rules. I think Aristotle liked things which followed the laws of nature. I think Aristotle didn't feel real good about automobiles or in-laws or the stock market which follow no natural law (nor no law at all, perhaps). I did not master nature on the mountain, but I did, necessarily learn to live with nature. I did not master human fickleness and variability when I was a child, nor when I met the many aspects of my dearest friends. I do not know that nature is easy to deal with, nor unnatural human behavior impossible. I shall try to learn.

I stride toward the center, hungry but full of each bit I perceive of this full little bit of the world natural and unnatural, this overwhelming fullness which cannot be perceived, this beautiful chaos which beloved Ari could order in his mind (but he couldn't rule the weather).

2. Whatever

And there's a little good in the worst of us, and a little of each of us in each of us. So I can understand you, and you can understand me. It can be done if we are willing. And I am learning to be willing.

I stride to the center of the city. It is mid-afternoon. Business as usual. Congested streets, congested sidewalks. Not so obvious from the street that all these towers are full of professionally compulsive and/or ebulliently engaging persons on telephones, filing papers, having serious meetings with each other, and each and every one with her or/and his very own CRT, keyboard, mouse, modem and printer. That makes . . . let's see . . . at least fifty skyscrapers here, average, say, thirty-four floors . . . twenty offices—no, say sixteen a floor . . . two girls for every boy . . . seventeen desks . . . That makes a whole lot of microelectronic equipment. And the persons, are they microelectronic? I trust not. I trust they are just who they are, and I don't know, because I haven't met them.

I would like to eat but I have no way to do it now. Now I must deal with a someone so I will be able to eat. I am here, where there are many persons, now who . . . ?

"Pardon, sir. I am hungry. Can you help me?"

"Beat it, bum."

"Good afternoon, ma'am. I am hungry. Can you help me."

"Touch me, I'll call a cop."

"Sir, I am new in town, haven't gotten started here yet. Can you help me get something to eat?"

"What are you up to? Leave me alone."

"Mister, I can use a favor."

He crosses the street against the light. I am learning this approach may not work, too straight forward, perhaps.

Carousel. I hadn't seen that sign by light of day. Much has changed with me since then, but it is what I recognize. I've learned to follow what I recognize. I trust I shall survive as long as I trust.

"Hi, buddy. What can I get you?"

"I'm hungry. Please feed me."

"Here's a menu. We're out of pork roast. You want a drink?"

"No, thank you, I don't drink any more."

"Well, what'll it be?"

"I have no money. I need something to eat, but I have no money."

"That's okay. I can use a little help."

"You mean I can work for something to eat? Good. So many people seem not to want to help me at all."

"No sob stories. I've heard them all. They're just not entertaining any more. Go down to the basement and bring up twelve cases of beer from the cooler. They're already stacked up. You can't miss the right ones. After you work I'll let you have a cheese sandwich and a beer."

"I don't drink any more."

"Whatever."

3. Re-Enter Society

I realize I have begun to re-enter society. I realize some will call this the bottom, but for me there is no longer a top or a bottom, no better or worse, only what is, here and now. And now I have eaten, have accomplished something for myself today. Perhaps I can accomplish something for someone else as well.

"Did I carry the cases of beer okay?"

"Yeah. Just fine."

"Is there something else I can do for you?"

"Look, I offered you a sandwich for a little errand. I didn't offer you a career position. If you want a job go to the day labor pool with all the other professionals between assignments."

He even tells me where, who is in charge. I follow signs, directions, instructions, intuitions. I trust.

"Lucky, are you? You're supposed to be here at seven a.m. sharp to get a job. There were at least twenty guys this morning I had to turn away. But here is a job unloading freight cars that just came up. You can go with these three guys, now. You stay until the job is done, probably midnight if you work fast. Five dollars an hour, cash, when you get done. If you don't finish you don't get paid."

Shorty is six foot four, Curly is completely bald and Hotshot is a severely slow superannuated punch-drunk pugilist. They are my partners. I like them.

Bags of concrete weigh ninety pounds. It could be worse, I am told. Some bags of some things weigh a hundred and fifty. Or it could be manure.

Repetitive tasks are difficult until you get the rhythm, or if you break the rhythm. When the car is full the bags are near the door, and we each carry one at a time to the pallets on the dock. As the car is more empty we wordlessly agree to form two-man relays to bring the bags across the car, then to the dock. When we finish the first car we take a break, and I feel fine, not sore or stiff at all. Starting the second car is a change in rhythm, and it is not like starting the first, for we are not exactly the same as we were. Before, we were fresh (or freshish), but after the break I am immediately stiff. The first car has taken us a little over three hours. The second feels slower.

There is a lesson in anything, and there is reassurance in reality no matter how negatively it can be read. Attitude counts. Hotshot isn't completely unaware. He must feel about like I do now, tired, stiff, sore, weak. "Fuck it," and he's gone. No pay? Another consideration entirely. The composition of my two-man relay has been altered somewhat. I am a one-man relay. Talking to myself may be crazy, but answering myself (I am told) is insanity. Arguing with myself must be utter lunacy. Performing a relay with myself works as poorly. I persist because I said I would. When they have finished their half of the second car Curly and Shorty sit back for a smoke. I understand what is happening without much difficulty, but I don't know how to respond to the wordless message. It occurs to me that they can read the situation as well as I, and that if they can't I can't instruct them better than to continue what I am doing. At least I know what I am doing—I am unloading a boxcar of cement, my (pardon me) concrete task. Simple repetitive tasks are easy to continue, but tend to have one talking to oneself. As long as one is answering merely it is not so bad. But I am tempted to argue with myself.

When I have finished my task I wake Curly and Shorty from their naps atop the sacks. We return to headquarters where Ralph is waiting.

"Midnight exactly. Good enough. Stacked straight, Curly? Where's Hotshot? Run out again? I'll bet I know who got stuck with him, right, Curly? Shorty? Okay, Kenneth, you've been initiated by the boys. That's why I said midnight, 'cause Hotshot can't stick with a long job. I wouldn't have sent him, but that's all I had at the time. You did these two boys a big favor, doing Hotshot's work for them. If you hadn't come by it would have been just the three of them . . . that is, the two of them. I imagine you did about half of Hotshot's work, so I'll give you about half his pay. I'll pay him his part tomorrow when he comes for it. At least he won't be hung over tomorrow; no money, no booze."

"Ralph, I just got to town, and now I'm really tired. I need a place to sleep."

"A lot of the guys sleep under the dock at the train yard. It's cheap enough."

"I think I've been there recently."

"There's the Chilton. If you can't find a clerk, just go up and down the hall until you find a bed, and pay them in the morning. But pay them, 'cause once you stiff someone on the street no one will have anything to do with you. The grapevine is powerful, like I already know where you dined for lunch, and what you ate— but I didn't hear about you until after I had sent you out on the job. It isn't 'cause I trusted you. Hell, I didn't figure anyone would steal a bag of concrete."

"You mean I've just been here since this afternoon, and already everyone knows me?"

"And you'll know absolutely everyone who's anyone by day after tomorrow."

4. A Monument

The Chilton doesn't look so bad to me. Simple, plain. Quite a bit worn. It must be an easier place to rest than under the dock. No one at the card table in the stairwell, not after midnight. The sign says so. It makes sense.

These are the creaky stairs up I never climbed. Not so easy a climb, my legs stiffer with each step. I had been a fairly limber mountain man, but two boxcars of cement, enough to make a monument to someone or something. Step, each step, another step. But, I opine, it has been step by step I have gone up and down, learned what little I know, survived by no power of my own except to move, to be flexible enough to go another step. I have learned to move as I am moved, not to resist, to go with the flow. I do not do it always, but when I do not I feel that I am not doing it, and I do not resist for long currents stronger than I can be. And when I will not follow what leads me I know I will be abraded by the rocky shoals or sticks along steep banks which reach out, tree roots and branches to snag me. And I let go again and float free, remembering it is this living river who knows where she goes, not I, happy little flotsam though I am.

Up the stairs is easier once I have reminded myself I don't know where I'm going. Down the hall the doors all look closed. I was told to find a bed. Following instructions I am brave. Maybe no one else will believe it, but I do, that I am innocent, not stealing purses. Lightly lean against a door. It does give. Again, lightly. Move along to the next door. Firm. The next, opens noisily. Glance into the grimy dark. Three bunks, lumps in each upper and lower berths. Pull the door back to, quietly as is impossible. Room 210, door locked (or frozen). The last room down this hall. Two bunks, five lumps.

Another flight of stairs. I am too tired and stiff to feel, but I feel fine. Hazy, but fine. After a time I am on the third floor. I try each door as politely as cannot be done. There seems no bed for me on the third floor.

On the way to the fourth floor I remember that there was a time at which I would have considered this behavior and this circumstance to be insane. I would have been at an elegant hotel paying plenty and not giving that a thought. I would have service, and propriety and privacy, and mild (purchased) adulation. Now I consider all that insanity. Resources are rare. Persons must share. The motivation is completely different—then I wanted attention, now I want rest. I need rest; I do not need attention.

Carefully but thoroughly I confirm the fourth floor is not for me tonight. So, to the fifth, for I shall follow instructions as well as I can, and I still can. At the top of the stairway is not an open hall darkened by a single meager bulb. Instead, at the top of the stair there is a doorway under which flows a stream of light. I am not reluctant to try the door, for I am following instructions. I turn the knob, I push, it gives.

5. Welcome

"Red!"

"Hi."

"Sorry to intrude."

"Come in."

"I was looking for a bed."

"There's one for you here. Sit down. You look tired."

"I am."

"I am too."

"I can't sit here. I can't stay here. Everything is so neat and pretty, and I am caked in cement."

"You're the first person to come in here in a long time who has done a day's work. You're welcome. Please come in, I need the company. The bathroom is there. Fresh towels are in the cabinet. There's plenty of hot water, and soaps of every flavor. I prefer the jasmine, it's more delicate. The sandalwood is overwhelming. I don't recommend it. Well, get with it. You need a bath, so take a bath."

Now I have bathed. Weak though I am, I am pleased that half the stiffness was hardened concrete. I have allowed myself to float with the currents in the tub, rather than to grasp egotistic pretensions that I need no offers of kindness and help, grasp them in front of me like a small bath towel to hide my nakedness if someone were to walk in on me abruptly. What is called modesty may be egotism. I acknowledge my needs and appreciate another's generosity. Don't look a gift bath in the mouth.

"I don't recognize you. How do you know me?"

"Oh, you did me a favor a few months ago, gave me directions when I was lost."

"I still can't place you, to be honest. Did you have that beard then?"

"No, come to think of it I didn't. I forgot I have a beard this year. I don't have to look at me, you know."

"Well, shave it then. Give an old man an even break."

I have shaven, and my face feels fresh and smooth. I have come out of hiding. Red has prepared a simple snack, a feast in my eyes—and in my mouth and stomach.

"So, you're the guy! Am I glad to see you!"

"But we just met for a moment. How could you remember or care . . ."

"You have saved my life—or saved my boy's life."

"I don't understand what you are saying."

"That's not important. I understand what I'm seeing."

"You are happy to see me. When I walked in this room you were burdened, weighted down with something painful, your face down, your shoulders round, your step a shuffle, mumbling muffled voice despite an openness and kindness unlike the brashness I remember in you then. But then you were drunk."

"And that was my last drink, at least so far. I hope I never take another."

"Something dramatic must have happened then, but I don't know how it could have touched you. Some coincidence . . . ?"

"It was some coincidence, all right, and now that you show up I almost understand it. I guess it can't hurt to let you know, if . . ."

"'If . . .' ?"

"Look, I may not be thinking very well, but I feel okay about you. Were you really looking for a room downstairs? Why? Why are you here, this place, this time?"

"This is just where I got to. I don't know why."

"And all the beds were full downstairs, so that brought you here to me. Amazing. It just shows me again that I don't know a whole hell of a lot. I thought I was smart, and I was just drunk. I thought I was in charge of half the county, and I couldn't even remember to zip my own fly. Well, one thing that happened is I found a better way. When they arrested Rick for murder I was too stunned to take another drink. For days I just sat here stunned and angry. I told my lawyers to get him right out of there, and when they said they couldn't I was stymied. I sat here and didn't drink. For the first time in forty years I sat here, but instead of a glass and a bottle and staring at the wall I had no glass and no bottle, staring at the wall. When I unfroze I went to jail to see him, and I tried to bail him out, but they wanted more than I could get hold of, and I ain't poor. I left the jail and walked to a meeting, and I didn't even know it. I just wandered and got there, came to in a bunch of ex-drunks I used to drink with. Wondered where they'd gone. They understood what I couldn't, told me to leave it be. I couldn't. When I heard there was no body I knew I could get him out. I was ready to tear the jail down with my bare hands. Lawyers told me I couldn't spring him because an old lady saw it, and his own brother. When they told me Pongo was ready to talk, I laughed. He's never spoken a word. And then I heard him. They played me a tape, said it was the boy, and even though I had never heard him speak, couldn't possibly know how he would sound, I just knew that was his voice. It had to be. I thought I was crushed then, but when I went to the jail next, even though I never asked him, didn't want to know, Rick told me he did it, he stabbed that man who had been looking for Pongo, didn't know why but knew he had done it. And you are the man!"

6. Ghost

So, it seems, we have some things to talk about, some things in common. Red has told me a poignant story marked by seeming coincidence, striking coincidence. His life has pivoted on the events of that one day, more, perhaps, than on the day he was born. It is late, but I realize I have no office to attend at eight in the morning, and after my bath and meal I feel a bit more alive, a bit more attentive, so I am glad to listen, bashful but willing to respond.

"There was no body. Of course there was no body. No one got killed. You're here. But even Rick thought he had killed you. How can that be?"

"I was killed."

"But how can you be here? Are you a ghost?"

"I am very much alive. As a friend of mine once said, 'It feels too bad to be heaven and too good to be hell.'"

"How can you be alive if you were killed?"

"I don't know."

"Will you go to the courthouse with me when they open, tell them to let Rick go?"

"Yes."

"If you will, I will do anything, give you anything I have."

"I don't need anything, thank you."

"I don't know what's been happening with me. My whole life is changing, and sometimes turning upside-down in a moment, then turning upside-down in another direction the next moment. I used to be in control, then, to tell you the truth, I lost it. I drank for years—it was part of my business—and I never had any trouble. Then some time recently—maybe two years ago—I begin to lose it, can't get drunk, can't get sober. Can't keep track of stuff, lose track of whole nights, lose track of business. Lucky my son is able to handle things for me, but he's young and brash—but I was young and brash when I was young, and brash. And I thought I was a mellow drunk, a pleasant man, a conversationalist. After I stopped drinking last winter people began to level with me, told me they didn't like me, I was obnoxious when I drank, wasn't polite at all, made crude remarks, hurt people's feelings. My employees hadn't loved me loyally; they had cringed and tolerated me for their pay. They didn't leave me alone out of respect; they just wanted to get away from me, spent their time with each other, and in other people's joints. Before that night, that next early morning—You know, you were here, of course . . . of course—I had refused to see my businesses disintegrate, even though Rick had told me. I had refused to see my brain was gone. Then, when Rick was charged with murder—your murder— and when Pongo was taken by Child Welfare, and later when the court awarded custody to the old lady, and I saw other guys, younger guys, taking over my business on the street, and I can't even manage the two girls I have left, and I'm going to meetings and these guys are telling me to let it all go, that I'm in the right place, that it gets better. And it does. And it's not because you showed up so Rick can get out, although I'm not surprised, but I don't know why I'm not surprised. The point is, things have been getting better for me on the inside, and it's not whether business stinks or not, and it's not even whether my kid's in jail or not. It just gets better. I honestly thought my life was over, and maybe it should have been. And you bet I thought of shooting myself, or having one last fatal drunk, but I was afraid I might not die, might just hurt worse, be more hopeless than I already was. Well, I didn't die, and now I'm alive for the rest of my life, and I'm glad. And if things are bad, that's just the way it goes, and when things are good I'm thankful."

"I didn't die either. We've come a long way, Red."

"I didn't do a thing, just got out of the way, stopped making messes."

"Out of the way and on the path."

7. Pure Energy

Avalon County Courthouse, eight o'clock a.m. Sunlight is pure energy, no color of its own. Steps worn granite, solid, should be mush from all the traffic all these years since my mother was in grade school down the street a couple blocks. Solid. The courthouse steps do not move under my feet. My feet move. Lockstep with Red, parallel. Up the steps, solid, businesslike. Quiet, waiting to be directed in a non-standard situation. Willing to go with the turbulent flow of the bureaucrats. No problem, no distractions, no preconceived notions, only focused on one simple goal—to walk in two, to walk out three.

I am not surprised how cooly Red can handle this. I understand he has been shaky for a long time, but now he knows exactly what he's doing, intuitively handles the situation smoothly. I am not surprised when we are bounced from one office to another, for how often can it be the living corpse comes to withdraw a complaint of murder? Which department is supposed to handle it? Where is it in the policy and procedure manual?

I am not surprised when merely half way past noon, after having interrogated me at length about being myself, the assistant district attorney brings me and a very thick file to the district attorney himself. The office is almost sumptuous, the man presumptuous.

> "We believe you are who you say you are, but we haven't proven it."

> "I agree with you. I believe I am myself, but I haven't proven it."

> "Enough sarcasm, there. I'm used to dealing with you criminals. You can't get away with anything with me."

> "I am not a criminal."

> "Not technically, yet. I'll ask the questions here, and I'll decide what are the right answers. On the night of September fifth of last year you were . . ."

His attitude does not hurt my feelings, just makes it thicker to converse with him. It reminds me there are many different truths, that the set of truths which will help Rick be free is all that counts as far as I am concerned. That I really was killed, that it is a sort of mystery that I am alive again, that Rick's business with me was illicit—these sorts of things have no bearing on the matter at hand.

A clerk comes in with a piece of paper. The D.A. whispers a question. The clerk whispers an answer. I am tempted to whisper to myself, but for Rick's sake I refrain.

> "We have confirmed your finger prints and your voice print. We thought he had killed you, but obviously he hasn't. We haven't yet identified another victim. Don't worry—I think of everything. You likely enough are an accomplice planted to cover up the identity of the real victim, poor soul. Whatever you are up to, we are watching you closely, all of you. We are forced to release him for now. His father is at the detention center waiting for him. You may meet them there."

I have met them already, more than once. I'll take a walk instead, stride through the old part of this city.

8. Wonder

No wonder. I need not wonder now. I know. I am here where I came from to travel forward by coming back. If I were ten thousand miles from here I would still be where I came from, coming back. I have a sense of easy freedom because I am free. Like Rick will be.

Old buildings, new buildings, middle-aged buildings. It is interesting to me to see buildings which were new when I walked down these streets to school, many empty, deteriorated, even gone, none as it was. And it is interesting to me to see some buildings as they were which were old when I was young.

It is pleasant for me to see persons this bright light spring day. My head is light from lack of sleep, but I am more than just okay. And they are okay with me, every one. Here are winos in an alley, gathered behind a dumpster, haggling, bragging, ragging one the other, juggling a long brown paper bag, struggling it between them, "Fuggin' queer, give it here," slugging air, hugging, mugging when they see me look their way. Here are children on their way from school, young ones, a group of them, a veritable alphabet of colors, shapes of teeth (and absence of them), hairs (none combed or brushed), busyness (none rushed to get home when expected—maybe no one's there), each and all dragging noisily grating lunchboxes along the curb as they walk in the street facing traffic, too jaded as city kids to be afraid of automobiles, which have to follow rules (it is the law) when they, liberated minors, can walk any where and any way their feet will take them (call a cop, they'll squeal and run a dozen different ways). Here is the super market, the place where thousands around the

172

clock buy motor oil, appliances, fat-free ice cream, pins, pens, pans, magazines, turkey roasters, hair remover, polish remover, drain clog remover, vacuum cleaner bags, ground lamb, clams, dusting rags, dry-roasted peanuts, snuff, kiwi fruit, condoms, sweet potatoes, stamps, and . . . (you know how much more if you have been to the store) rent floor buffers and video tapes, where every sort of person comes all the time, fat ladies who strike their children, pale darned old men who study fruit, brusque laughing laborers who come for sandwiches and milk, young couples who shop together sharing his lessons on how to cook gourmet elegance, old couples who scrutinize the labels they can hardly read reminding one another how many cents this item was at another store or forty years ago so they can save a very few pennies, mothers of large families who whip down the aisles with two baskets unwavering grabbing the largest boxes and packages of exactly what they know they want or what their coupons specify . . . and you know this series of persons because it is us. Each group is us, each individual I.

I can't live in isolation. I must be able to see you standing there for me to see myself. It is mirroring, not confusion of identity. Identity is fluid enough for the very healthy and the very crazy. In the middle we get rigid. When I was alone on my mountain I learned from the source much of who I really am, how changeable I am and still remain exactly who I am this silly life so grave. But now, no matter that I am clumsy and uncomfortable about it, I need you. I am glad you are here with me on this pleasant walk.

9. Handsome

"Hey, Kenneth! Come here. We have been looking for you. Come on home and clean up. We're going out tonight. Rick is waiting to see you."

"Home?"

"Where we live, you fool, where we live."

Red puts his arm around my shoulders joyous. I feel his energy, his tears. I am not sure I understand our affinity now, remembering how repelling he was to me when we first met. We walk past the courthouse in the late afternoon, the gold orange glow before darkness who washes the face of the land cool and calming. Together we stride to the narrower streets where old tenements still stand in the shadows of the sky-scrapers. Sounds and smells and colors, movement of children, flapping in the air of hung laundry, slow booming of slow moving trucks, high pitched rattles of giant old blotched cars abraded of their paint, the crunching rumble of a freight train a few blocks away, and even chirps of birds: these are a smorgasbord of the sensual side of the substance of the city, a delicatessen cabinet offering almost too much of what has flavor and color, which can be taken in in mixtures of its richnesses, and no calories, no cholesterol. I do not romanticize. This is the reality: the world is full of lively beauty.

We approach the Chilton, and for the first time I see it in the light. It is a handsome building, not at all small filling half a small block. I had only entered at the open end, had never seen the wide main door boarded over, along the other street. Wondering takes no time at all. In no time at all I wonder if we all (or many of us) have boarded over the broad accesses to our living space, left only narrow side doors off of alleys to have others visit us, to come into our selves.

Into the side door and up the stairs. To the fourth floor, then the fifth.

"I had never noticed the front door of the hotel."

"It was a glorious place when I grew up here. Busy, too. My grandfather built the Chilton. I still own it, for what it's worth. Carriages arrived at that big door, and automobiles too, of course. Three presidents have stayed here, and a whole lot of hookers. I learned the hotel trade from the time I was a kid, and the prostitution trade, which is hardly different or more glamorous than any other. Work is work, and I really guess hardly anyone makes a living without working at it, but I also guess there is no work to do which can't be fun. Maybe someone will argue with me, but I've done a lot of kinds of jobs, and as long as I had a positive attitude I had fun."

"A fancy hotel, huh?"

"Real fancy, real fun. You gotta get dressed now, Kenneth. We have some real celebrating to do. I'm not well practiced at celebrating with soda water, but I'm ready to give it a try. You gotta get dressed now."

"Dressed? I am dressed. These are all the clothes I have. I'm dressed."

"You're not a lot smaller than me, or a lot larger than Rick. We've got plenty of clothes, and you're welcome to have any of them. Tomorrow, if you need new clothes, we'll take you to the fanciest stores in town, the Fandango Boutique and the European Specialty Company. Right now get dressed. I told Rick to get Monica and Sibel and meet us at Cliff Young's. I used to be able to afford places like that. Some day I will again."

10. Clothing Which Almost Fits

I have done well to find clothing which almost fits me . . . done well, that is, until I have come to a frightening snakes' nest of neckties, each too broad or narrow, too brilliant a green, too grease-stained, purply spotted, streaked in gold, and one (I swear) painted fluorescent with a naked lady. I decide to wear Rick's collar open.

Red and I walk southeast, across the imaginary line which separates high class from low life. A few moments, a few blocks, and we are walking past tuxedoed valet parking attendants who are looking for our car. The door swings open for us, held by Cliff Young himself, not so young as he once was, bearded, slightly portly, but a youthful elan about him, not only entourage but energy. His calm bespeaks taste, not appetite. As we enter the hybrid Victorian/Art Deco restaurant, more than the clash of Leroy Nieman paintings against exuberant floral arrangements, more than the clash of the excellently dressed who have driven their Jaguars against the nearly naked children in the tenements across the street—more than these external disjunctions, I hear the static clatter within me, the old pleasures I puffed myself up with walking into such places, the recent pleasures I have had in modest solitude starving on the mountain growing through the winter—and I realize my state of soul as I walk in here now, that I am neutral, all about me is just the way it is, and it is all right with me as long as I am all right.

Who is with me is all right, Red the rough street entrepreneur, my old acquaintance, my new brother, raised in elegance, seasoned in whiskey, twin of Hunter S. Thompson, widower of Norma Jean

Baker, father of my murderer, enslaver of my child, my host and friend. We will meet with others: Rick whom I know and whom I bear no malice, Sibel and Monica (Monica? Do I know a Monica?), and I have no idea who else.

Cliff Young quietly directs us to the red-flocked ornately patterned wallpaper and red velvet curtained and upholstered private dining room between the main restaurant and the gaudy nightclub Ruby. Noise filters through the mouseholes in the wall, the band on the hellish podium next door, not especially disturbing, but clearly whispering of fish net stockings serving champagne cocktails. Neutral and accepting in my heart, I am also excited to see who will be here with us. Three figures stand, sip and chat at the far end of the room. I recognize Rick, slick, a bit thinner for his time in jail, glib, entertaining the two others, a pert dark nodding quiet one and the lithest whitest one I ever saw once before (but not in some light) gesticulating histrionically, pointing to herself, to the heavens and the whole wide world, and back again to her self.

"Rick, how does it feel to be really free?"

"Just fine, Dad. Superb."

"Monica, Sibel, this is a special friend of ours, our guest of honor. I want you to treat him as one of the family. For me he is. He's like the little brother I never had. You may not know, but when I was a kid we were really rich, not just from the Chilton but from a lot of other properties my family owned. They gave me anything I wanted, but the one thing I wanted they wouldn't give me was a little brother. The one thing I wanted was a little brother, and since they wouldn't give me what I wanted then, I'll let myself have it now. Kenneth, will you be my little brother?"

"Charmed."

"Monica, meet Kenneth."

"I feel we've met before, Monica."

"Most men say that, and most men are right. Hi, honey."

"Sibel . . ."

(As she tips her drink in leaning forward, pours a bit on her shoe) "Whoopsie."

"I'm pleased to meet you, Sibel."

"And you know Rick."

"Kenneth, look, there's something I want to say to you . . ."

"Not necessary, Rick. I have no problem with you."

"But I think I have a problem, a big one . . ."

"If you can wait . . ."

"I hate to wait for anything, but this I have put off for too long already, so a little longer may be okay. But, Kenneth, soon?"

"Soon. I'm thirsty."

"Me, too. Let me order you a drink, seven different secret fruit juices and no rum. People may not recognize me sober, but I don't care. And I'll bet they don't care either. Rick, what are you drinking?"

"Ah, er, really? Soda water with a squeeze of lime. Easy on the lime."

"Girls?"

"We'll stick with champagne, Red. Fruit juice would shock our systems."

Such a setting. Such relationships, difficult to describe. Such anticipation of who shall fill . . . Let me count the places at the table . . . Eight set . . . And who shall fill the other three?

11. Did You Have Sex?

We chat honestly and comfortably, sip punch, stand glancing out the window, silently note the outlandish garb and faces of those ushered from limousines by driver and parking attendant and doorman all at once. Most of the drivers nowadays are women. They may be more attentive to the delicate needs of their fares. Most of the limousines are white, although a few are black, but a few are pastel colors, too. Entertaining mildly, but things seem unimportant compared to the intricate realities of persons.

"How were things in jail this time, Rick?"

"How it is always, I suppose, but this time longer. I always got out quicker before. Not that it has been so often, only three times. But nine months! It's long enough to have a baby."

"Did you have sex?"

"No, Monica, I didn't have sex. Is that all you think of? I suppose I would have had sex whether I wanted to or not, but they kept me isolated. Red came every day, but they only let me see him once a week, for ten minutes. Mostly I thought and read. Believe it or not I read Aristotle, and a lot of other things, too—Hunter S. Thompson and Kurt Vonnegut and a little Kierkegaard. I was afraid to read Hesse, alone and all. I thought a lot, but I can't remember what I thought. When I was reading the author gave some sense to what I was reading, but when I was the author, in my imagination, I couldn't make much sense of it. I guess I need a teacher to hold my hand when I try to think. But I am glad to be free now, and it is tempting never to think again. But now that I have tried, I think I'll have to keep trying to think, whether I want to or not. There was a time I thought all I had to do was hustle, make money, party and die, but now I know there's more. I don't know what it is, but there is more for me. I don't know what the answer is right now. I used to have an answer for everything, a great big lie, and I got away with it most of the time. But now I feel there is some simple truth I don't know yet, and I feel like I'm going to find it. I'm not going to write a book about it, but I'm going to do something, and it's not going to be alone (like writing a book) but something with other people, 'cause I get along with people (I'm a people person), but instead of lying to them (like selling used cars) it's got to be something true, like doing something with them, building something."

"Hors d'ouvres?"

"Thanks. Delicious."

"Kenneth, where have you been? What have you been doing?"

"Oh, just the same as Rick. I've had no sex. I have been in isolation. I had visits from some of my 'family', but that didn't keep me from being alone. I have read a little (and am afraid of Hesse). I have thought a lot, but I don't know what that adds up to. I, too, feel the need for a Mentor to guide me. There is some sort of truth or ringing-true I wish to live with every moment, but I have no power to possess it all by myself. I have been set free again in society, and although I am happy to be just as I am, there is something (I do not know what it is) I need to do with other persons, with a community of persons."

12. Deep Joy

Each of us has heavy experiences, heavy aspirations. These do not preclude light conversation. We accept isolation, imprisonment, alienation, madness as dinner conversation no less than new washing machines, golf swings, PTA meetings. All human experience is valid.

We chat and glance out the window. A very large gold limousine docks like a large yacht at the entrance to Cliff Young's. Slowly out of it emerge, attended by the driver in her miniskirt, two parking attendants, the doorman and Cliff Young himself, a large old woman creaky in her joints, slow, clumsy at maneuvering her legs and purse through even so large a door, and a small boy obedient and wonder-struck. They are my companion and Pongo! It is as I saw them coming across the meadow, and I know my heart is home with them, as if they were bringing it to me in the large ornately wrapped and ribboned box the boy carries.

My deep joy to see you, beloved friend. She arthritically makes her way across the crowded lounge and bar into the room where we await them. In her flowered dress, her clunky healthy shoes, her gold-rimmed glasses, her purse swinging from her elbow, she looks more like a Jewish grandmother than Woody Allen's fantasies of a Jewish grandmother, more like a Jewish grandmother than my guru.

> "Franklin, I heard Rick was released, so I called Social Services and they said we could come back, so here we are. How are you?"

"Madge! Oh, my favorite Madger. Here's Rick, all in one piece. Here I am, all in one lump. You know Monica and Sibel. And this is Kenneth, our guest of honor. And Pongo! Always our guest of honor. And Rick may as well be our guest of honor also. So I guess we have enough guests of honor . . . Oh! One more, Cliff Young, poet, critic, restaurateur. Come, Cliff. Here, next to the head of the table. This time I'll hold your chair."

We are seated, although I am tempted to continue mingling, so many questions, so many lingering looks, so many hugs remain undone. I am at the far end, Pongo opposite me at the head flanked by Mister Young and Grandma Badger. The two women sit on my each side, Monica and Sibel. In the middle, facing each other through a flamboyant bouquet of mountain wild flowers and crooked sticks, sit Red and Rick, father and son together again.

Silently to myself I shake my head and laugh at what it all is— events, relationships, coincidences, times and places interwoven as if the only stability might be in my human heart, the meanings which shower like sparks from the brushing together of all that is beyond me with whatever is within me. Certainly convention and society are more orderly than all this, but they seem lost to me. What I have is what is real for me, no matter how mad it may seem. It is beginning to seem just fine to me, because I have set aside any expectations. I am so much luckier getting what I need instead of what I want. I toast

"To all that is!"

13. Whoopsie!

It is decorous dining not only because of the decor but especially because of the decorum. At first snails, and ceviche of venison. Salad is leaves of every color, peppers of varying flavors, nuts—pinon, walnut, pistachio, almond—roasted or toasted, straw mushrooms, jicama julienned—and I find myself digging for maple bark. The dressing is raspberry vinegar and eel oil seasoned with fresh ginger and cayenne. Hot breads are sweet with cinnamon, savory with dill, aromatic with orange zest, penetrating with jalapeno. Sibel and Monica drink champagne and more champagne, but just a sip at a time. Red and Rick and Madge drink Red's special rumless punch. Pongo has soda pop, I black coffee. Mister Young, emotionally entwined in our communal spirit grasps a large tumbler of cold gin with both hands. He remains reserved. We intermingle toasts as we wish, messages shared to celebrate each other.

> "To Pongo, our favorite boy. A speech, Pongo, a small speech from a small person."

> "Unaccustomed as I am to speak, you know I love each of you. I am happy to be here. I have heard you say sometimes that I have had a hard childhood. Well, it certainly has been long. But I want each of you to know it has not been so hard, or no harder than I imagine anyone else's childhood likely would be. Mostly I have been alone. Isolation brings hope, sometimes, but it also brings mistrust. I have been blessed with hope in my loneliness, because I have not hated or blamed me for the painful experiences. I have not hated or blamed

anyone, just waited and hoped, and numbed myself against what I couldn't understand or stand at all. I have waited for each person who is important to me—each of you—and now I am with you. You have put me at the head of the table not to humor a child, but to honor a friend who loves you, who hopes his love will help you hope, not hate. This is enough of a speech from a speechless boy. If you wonder that I seem used to words, please remember I also have lived in them as long as each of you. This child does not hate you. The child within each of you does not hate you. Life is too full to leave room for hating. I love you."

And the soup, redolent with jasmine whose blossoms float in its little ocean, is a simple broth of crab, one of which entire swims in each bowl, a lazy natator in a pool on a hot summer day, the little sunglasses a decorative touch which would never come about except at Cliff Young's.

"To Red, again the leader of this clan, the leader we need, we who have been each wandering."

"I'm beginning to learn, now that I'm beginning to pay attention. I am really ready to cry realizing how each of you has stayed loyal to me when I was impossible to tolerate. Until I sobered up I didn't know how I had slipped, or when. Monica, Sibel, you kept my business going when all the rest had gone. You kept me from starving, when I was supposed to be keeping you."

Red raises his glass of fruit juice, Monica and Sibel their tulips of champagne. Sibel tips her glass, tipsy, dribbles wine in her lap.

"Whoopsie!"

Red resumes as the sorbet of buffalo hump is served in a bed which is a magnolia blossom.

"Pongo, it is true I saved you once, but you don't owe me. (I just wanted to remind myself I had done something good, a long time ago.) The last few years the way I used you has been pretty awful. I can't make up for it, but I won't do it again. If there is anything at all I can do to make up for even a little part of it, speak right out and tell me now that you can speak). Madge, you have stayed with me the longest, and I don't know why. When you married me I was an energetic young hotelier, an attentive husband. As conditions worsened rapidly I took to gambling, thinking I could instantly recuperate our fortune, but I ran things downhill faster. We survived, it is true, but the work I did has been sordid, and you have somehow stayed above it all. I have resented that, thinking you were haughty, but now I see you were doing what you had to do to care for me and Rick and Pongo. I swear you are a spiritual superman . . . er, superwoman . . . er, superperson, I guess is the proper way to say it nowadays. I'll never repay you, but I thank you from the bottom of my heart."

Which is exactly the moment at which the serene diminuitive Bébé serves the piéce de résistance (Pongo's favorite gourmet meal)—heart-shaped sandwiches of cashew butter and molasses between raisin bread, candied yams, candied carrots, stewed prunes all arranged (or painted) on the plate in exact replicas of Micky Mouse, a different pose on each diner's plate.

"To Rick, to freedom. Speak, Rick."

"I'm sure glad to be out of jail, ah gay-ron-tee. I gotta tell my dad I really thank him for sticking with me. He always has stuck with me, and he's always been my hero, so I kinda have taken it for granite, and this time I'm gonna say it out loud. Thanks, Red. Freedom . . . well, I never gave that a thought either, thought I was free as a bird. I don't want to be free to pick up where I left off. (Sorry, girls.) I need to grow, build and grow. I want to see something come from my own hands, and not to own it but just to have it in my heart. I've thought a lot. I thought I didn't know what I was thinking in jail, but now it becomes more clear: I thought, 'Rick, you haven't been doing anything with your life but chasing venereal disease and hangovers. You're lucky you're not an airplane pilot, 'cause you'd crash for sure. As it is, you're crashing slowly. You need to give something instead of grabbing all the time. Give something to someone else so you can be okay someday. Who do you care about you could give something to? Red, of course. What does he need? What does he want? What does he have already? Well, he doesn't have anything except the old broke down Chilton. And what he wants is to feel good about hisself like he did once. So, Rick, fix the Chilton.' That's what I thought, and that's what I'm going to do."

(Cheers.)

"Whoopsie!"

Dessert: quadruple chocolate tort, sauce apricot flambé, and avocado ice cream as a little misdemeanor. Bébé expertly arcs the flames just to the ceiling.

"I want to make a toast now," tears in his impassive eyes welling. "To all of you, who are such a touching family. To each of you, whose tenderness and bravery touch me. To Red, who is the first customer ever to make me a guest at his table. To Rick, who will build me an elegant restaurant in the new Chilton. To Pongo, whose taste in food is as delicate as my own. To Kenneth, who will be the last person to come into Cliff Young's without a tie. To Madge, who reminds me of my grandmother and my first wife. But especially to you, Sibel and Monica, who will be the sweetest dessert I have ever eaten!"

Whereupon he clears the table with a single sweep of his arm, fire in his eyes, and even before the tinkling crash has died, Cliff Young sweeps up in his arms two giddy prostitutes, lays them on the naked table, and with gluttonous gurgles, jaws jiggling, attacks their giggling girdles, they juggling unsuccessfully their wine.

"Whoopsie!"

"Gr-ow-wo-or!"

Bébé and Ivan the parking attendant quietly lead away the rabid Mister Young, who has for the first time in his own restaurant raised his voice after sundown.

"I'll sue you for this! I swear I'll sue you, you gonzo journalist!"

14. Midnight

A rare clear night in Avalon, stars singing angel songs. Seven abreast we walk the empty streets at midnight lockstepped, laughing.

"Okay, which of you is the gonzo journalist?" (All confess spontaneously.)

"Everything is nicer than ever it was."

"It is midnight. Now tomorrow is today. So, what shall we do today?"

"Let's see . . . Let's build a hotel."

"Now there's a nice one to start with."

"But that's the Chilton."

"That's our Chilton."

"Dad, I'm serious. I remember hearing you talk about it when I was a kid. You may not remember because you may have been a little drunk."

"I may have been drunk a lot."

"I remember what the Chilton was like a long time before I was born because I could feel it in how you felt, how you looked to me, what you said. I knew you wanted to fix it up, but we never had anything, never could get any money, so I kinda forgot about it too. But this time in jail I had time, and I finally realized what we need isn't money. We need me! I'm gonna do it, Red."

"Not by yourself, you're not. You're not doing this without us. Sibel and I are sick of acting. It's time for us to change professions. She can be a bookkeeper again, and I can use all my acting experience on the phone—and when we open the new hotel, I shall be the madam."

"And I shall be the bellboy, 'cause I ain't a prostitute any more."

"No, you ain't, Pongo. Never again. And please don't say 'ain't'."

"And, Kenneth, you'll stay with us, won't you, Kenneth? It's a family, Kenneth, and your part of it. It's a family project and we need you."

"Franklin?"

"Yes, Madge."

"You will need money to do this. You can have loyalty and élan, sweat and skill, from your son, your friends, but you need materials at least, and to buy more labor than the seven of us can make, and maybe even an architect or a contractor who knows which inspectors can be bribed."

"She's never wrong, Red. She has advised me with nothing but shrugs, and she's never wrong. She has infuriated me by being right, but she's never wrong, Red."

"Nor are we wrong now, nor will we be wrong tomorrow, nor ever again. We are together, we see our purpose, and especially we are happy with each other, with who we are and what we are doing. To hell with perfection—wonderful is good enough for me."

15. Together

And it is. It is all there is. Oh, Ari, when we tried to dichotomize we meant well, but everyone misunderstood. We meant to make more clear all that is, to rejoice, to live in it. But it was too easy for people to read it as the polarization of good and bad, us and them, right and wrong. They took it as a justification to segregate black from white, when all we meant to do was to illuminate the zillion different shades of grey. Societies don't exist, but they have used anything we have said against us, against each other. Our well-meant scholarship hasn't helped us live. It has not been so wonderful as we have wished.

But this is. Of all that is, this now is the most supremely existent. The simple feeling of our being together is worth the whole of suffering, counterbalances whatever may seem bad, gives positive meaning to what had seemed evil. Living fully and together justifies scholarship and every other thing which otherwise will be tedious or misleading. Laying bricks is concrete joy. Smiling and singing are no longer acting or counterphobia. Never perfect, but every day is something wonderful.

And I recognize what in my isolation I learned in my heart. No one of these persons is my mere fantasy. I live and work with them without suspicion or rancor because I no longer relate to others through fear and anger I had denied. Each one is real, and my love and trust come in great part from my knowing each of them in my heart, identifying within myself the parts of me with which they resonate.

Madge remains a wise, supportive friend.

The boy's joy thrills me as I cannot thrill myself.

Monica is energetic, effervescent—and it is no act, but who she is. Accepting her spontaneity allows me to share that energy.

Rick and I work together wordlessly. We align beams with our eyes mirroring each other from each end, fit them with our heads side to side glancing, forth and back squinting, lift them into place, bolt them tight, together wordlessly.

It is easier today to sleep than ever in my life, and to rest. It is easier to sleep with Monica, to rest even when we talk all night, don't sleep. When we are awake together perhaps we are dreaming, for it is a dream. Now I never leave where I live, whom I live with. I am with Monica waking and sleeping, and I am building the Hotel Chilton sleeping or waking. My life is not possessed by nor preoccupied with my family, but filled by them. I forget the beginning of belonging; isolation and alienation of weeks ago no longer exist nor are remembered. I know the end now, the *telos* and the *finale*. It is now.

> "Hey, you two grownups, wake up! It's been morning all day long. Gramma Madge says we've all worked hard enough this week, so we're going to the mountain meadow for a picnic—and Grampa Red is going to teach me how to catch fish!"

The mountains look different every time I come to them. They, also, are alive and ever-changing. Today they are emeralds, amber and crystal as we laugh our way up the road in the old pickup truck. My icy mountain death has left me. Alive, I rejoice in all who are with me, all that is before me.

So, for me, you see, this is all there is. This is all I need. Good luck to you, my friend.

FINIS